Boyds will be Boyds

DANGER! BOYS DANCING!

Boyds will Be Boyds™

DANGER! BOYS DANCING!

by Sarah weeks

AN
APPLE
PAPERBACK

SCHOLASTIC INC.

New York Toronto London Auckland Sydney
Mexico City New Delhi Hong Kong Buenos Aires

For Gina Shaw — because she's just such a pleasure to work with!

— S.W.

CONTENTS

CHAPTER ONE

A lot of stories start off with somebody walking down the street, minding their own business when out of the blue — *bam!* — something unexpected happens to them and suddenly everything changes. It's true, a lot of stories start that way, but this doesn't happen to be one of them.

This story starts out in my backyard, with Fink and me sitting up in our favorite tree, eating cheese crackers and dill pickles one afternoon after school. We were talking, which shouldn't come as a surprise to anybody who knows us, because when we're together, it seems like we never run out of things to talk about.

"What do you think the surprise is?" he asked me.

"She didn't say surprise," I corrected. "She said *special treat*."

"So what do you think the special treat is?" he asked.

"Hard to tell," I said. "It sort of depends on whether she means special to *her* or special to *us*."

"What do you mean?" asked Fink.

"Well, do you think cutting your toenails is special?" I asked.

"Hello? What kind of question is that?" said Fink. "Of course I don't think cutting my toenails is special."

"Does your mom?" I asked.

"How should I know? She gets it done down at the beauty parlor," said Fink.

"Yep. Mine too. It's called a pedicure," I said. "Does your mom get dressed up when she goes to have it done?" I asked.

"I never really thought about it, but I guess she does. What's your point?" asked Fink.

"My point is, the reason they get dressed up is because they think going to get their toenails cut is *special*," I said.

Fink's eyes got really wide.

"You don't think Mrs. West is planning to get us all pedicures for our special treat, do you?" he asked.

"Don't be dumb," I said.

"Suck your thumb," he replied.

"Not now," I said.

"Milk a cow," said Fink.

"No, for real, Fink. *Not now*. I don't feel like playing the rhyming game," I told him. Fink and I have invented a lot of games over the years.

"You used to love that game. How come you don't like to play anymore, Nat-man?" Fink asked me.

"I don't know. I guess maybe I've outgrown it," I said.

"Oh, well, *excuse* me for being so *immature*," said Fink.

"Ugh, you sound like Marla," I said with disgust. "She loves that word, *immature*."

Marla Dundee and her evil twin, Jessie Kornblume, are the two most annoying girls in our class. Actually, make that the two most annoying girls *in the world*.

"What if the special treat is something girly?" said Fink, wrinkling his nose.

"Like what?" I asked.

"Like making valentines out of doilies," said Fink with disgust.

"Valentine's Day is ages away. Why would we be making valentines now?" I asked.

"I was just using that as an example of a girly thing," Fink explained. "You know, glitter and frills and mushy love junk."

"Speaking of mushy love junk, how's Leslie Zebak?" I asked.

Fink groaned.

"Why are girls so dense?" he asked. "Haven't I made it totally clear that I'm not interested in her?"

"Totally," I said.

"Then why does she keep writing me love notes?" asked Fink.

"I guess she's stuck on you," I said.

"I wish she'd get stuck on a big wad of gum instead," said Fink.

I popped a cheese cracker in my mouth, leaned back against a thick branch, and munched quietly for a while.

"So, I've been thinking about a hairless rat," I finally said.

"Can we please get off the topic of Leslie Zebak?" asked Fink.

"No, seriously," I said. "I've been thinking about buying myself a hairless rat. Wouldn't that be cool?"

"Uh, well, I guess a rat would be sort of cool to have as a pet, but does it have to be a bald one?" asked Fink.

"Yeah, because of my mom," I said.

"Oh, right," said Fink. "I forgot."

I have a pet. Hercules, my goldfish. He's a nice fish, and I like him just fine, but basically all he does is eat, blow bubbles, swim around, and mess up his fishbowl. It's not all that exciting to watch after a while. A dog would be the perfect pet. I could teach

5

him all kinds of tricks, and he could sleep on my bed at night. A dog would be great, except that my mom's allergic to anything with fur. That's how I came up with the idea of the hairless rat.

"They've got them down at Purr-fect Pets," I said, "and they're only ten bucks."

"*Ten bucks?* You can get a newt for two dollars and fifty cents. And they're *supposed* to be bald," said Fink.

"Newts are cool, but they can't do tricks," I said. "You can teach rats all kinds of things. They're really smart."

"Do you think you could teach your bald rat how to get rid of Leslie Zebak for me?" asked Fink, reaching for a cracker. "That would certainly be worth ten bucks."

Later, we went inside to work on our homework together. Fink and I are both pretty smart, but not at the same things. Fink is better at math and history and I'm better at science and writing. If you could just put us together, we'd be downright brilliant.

Anyway, we were working on our American history homework assignment when the subject of Mrs. West's special treat came up again.

"What if it's something great like a field trip to Splash-o-Mania?" said Fink.

"That would be cool! Have you seen the new ad for it on TV?" I asked.

"*The Slide of Death — takes your breath away and never gives it back!*" Fink and I both said together, imitating the deep voice of the guy in the commercial.

"Jinx on Froozles!" Fink shouted, punching me in the arm. This was another one of our games.

"Ow!" I said, rubbing my arm. "Fine. You win. How many does that make?"

"You owe me twenty-seven," he said.

Fink always wins the Jinx on Froozles game, but so far he hasn't made me pay up. It's a good thing, since I only get three bucks a week for my allowance, and Froozles — which are these giant milk shakes with frozen cookies mixed in — cost three-fifty down at the Bee Hive snack bar. I can't afford to go into debt buying milk shakes right now. Not when I'm saving up for my hairless rat.

"Maybe the special treat is a pizza party," said Fink.

"Why would Mrs. West give us a pizza party *now*?" I asked. "Teachers only give pizza parties when it's the end of the year or somebody in the class wins the citywide spelling bee or something big like that."

"Wait! I know what it is!" Fink said, throwing his arms up in the air so enthusiastically that he lost his balance and almost fell off his chair.

"What?" I asked, grabbing him by the elbow and pulling him back onto his seat.

"We're going to Washington," he said.

"Washington, D.C.?" I asked.

"Yeah, don't you remember? Mrs. West said we were going to be studying the White House this month. How can we study something we haven't ever seen?" Fink said.

"What are you talking about, Fink? We study all

kinds of things we've never seen," I said. "Remember Vasco da Gama? We studied him and we never saw him."

"How could we? He's dead," Fink said. "But the White House is alive and well in Washington, D.C., I'm telling you, we're going to Washington. That's the special treat, Nat-o. I'm positive."

"I'm not so sure," I said.

One thing I did know for sure was that pickles and cheese crackers made me really thirsty.

"You want some juice?" I asked, as I stood up and headed out to the kitchen. Fink followed me.

"They make money in Washington," Fink said.

"Yeah, I guess politicians get paid pretty well," I said.

"No, I mean they *make* money there. At the mint. You know, dollar bills and pennies and dimes. I read somewhere that you can take a tour of the place and actually see them making cash," he said.

"That would be awesome," I said.

"And the FBI is in Washington, too," Fink said.

"Wouldn't it be amazing to see them working on some top secret plan?"

"It wouldn't be very confidential if they let a bunch of fifth graders from Jeffersonville Elementary School in on it, would it, genius?" I asked.

"I guess not," Fink said, taking the glass of juice I'd poured for him.

"Hey, Nat-o, do you think there's any chance we'll get to meet the president when we go to the White House?" asked Fink.

"I don't know," I said. "I hope so."

"Not me," Fink said. "My parents didn't vote for him. That could be very embarrassing if it came up."

Fink stopped talking and looked longingly at the kitchen cupboards.

"Are you absolutely positive there aren't any cookies in there?" he asked. "Maybe an old box of stale Girl Scout cookies way in the back or something?"

I gave him a look. He knows my mother doesn't keep cookies in the house.

"You are what you eat," she always says. I've tried arguing with her about that.

"If I am what I eat, then don't you think you should let me eat sweets so that I'll be a sweet person?" I ask her.

"You might be sweeter, but your teeth would be full of cavities," she says, and that's usually the end of the discussion.

"I don't know how you can stand it," Fink said, as we carried our juice back out to the dining room, where our homework was spread out on the table. "I live for sugar."

Fink was about to take a gulp of juice, but when he noticed me scratching, he put down his glass and pointed at my leg.

"Uh-oh," he said. "What's that all about, Nat-o?"

In case you don't already know, my knee has this habit of itching whenever something bad is about to happen to me.

"Maybe it has something to do with going to Washington," Fink said. "Maybe something bad is going to happen on the trip."

"Great. We don't even know if we're going to Washington yet and you're already predicting something bad is going to happen to me there!" I said.

"Hey, don't blame me. I'm not predicting it, your knee is," Fink said.

Fink was right. My knee was definitely trying to tell me something, and whatever it was, I was sure it wasn't good.

CHAPTER TWO

"You have to come to Washington, no matter what," Fink told me the next day as we were standing in the yard at school, waiting for the first bell. "After what happened with me being sick for nature camp, there's no way we're not going to Washington together — itchy knee or not."

Fink stopped talking and stared at me.

"What's the matter?" I asked, looking down. "Did I forget to pull my zipper up all the way or something?"

"No. I was just noticing that you're not scratching anymore," he said.

"I was a little itchy this morning at breakfast," I told him. "But now I'm not."

Fink broke into a huge grin.

"Great! That must mean the bad thing is going to happen at home. If it was about the school trip, you'd be itching right now because you're at school," he said. "So, you see, there's nothing to worry about. We're going to Washington, Nat-man! Look out, America, the Boyds are hitting the capital!"

Sometimes Fink has a way of being so confident about things that you get the impression he knows what he's talking about even when he doesn't. The bell rang and we went inside. I'd been so busy thinking about my knee and the trip to Washington, D.C., that I had completely forgotten that it was the third Tuesday of the month. I got my memory refreshed in the form of a big wet spitball in the back of the neck.

"Ow!" I said, whirling around to face who had done it.

It was Mad Dog, of course. Mad Dog Ditmeyer gets his braces tightened on the third Monday of every month. Since my mother is his orthodontist, Mad

Dog has decided that the day after he sees her, if his teeth are hurting (which is pretty much guaranteed to be true the day after anybody gets their braces tightened), it's payback time. Since I'm related to her, *I'm* the one who has to pay the price. Not that he's particularly nice to me on any other day, but the third Tuesday of each month, he's really on my case.

I sighed and pulled the spitty wad of paper off my neck, tossing it in the trash can. The one thing I can say for Mad Dog is that he's consistent. Consistently mean, consistently gross, and consistently a big pain in the neck — sometimes literally.

"Do you think Mad Dog is ever going to stop being a jerk, or is he going to be like that forever?" asked Fink.

"You know what they say: A leopard cannot change his spots," I said. "It wouldn't surprise me a bit if Mad Dog ended up being like that mean old neighbor of ours, Mr. Baldwin. He throws rocks at squirrels when they climb on his bird feeders."

"You should tell Mr. Baldwin to use Vaseline instead," Fink said. "I read somewhere that if you smear it on the pole, it makes it too slippery for the squirrels to climb up."

"Does it work?" I asked.

"I doubt it. Instead of climbing up the poles, they'd probably just climb up the nearest tree and then jump onto the bird feeder," Fink said.

"Yeah, they're not as smart as rats, but squirrels are still pretty clever," I said.

Fink and I walked over to the classroom "post office" together where we each have a "mailbox" in which Mrs. West puts handouts and corrected homework papers. Fink reached into his box. As he pulled out a stack of papers, something square and pink slipped out and fell on the floor.

"Phew! What's that awful stink?" I asked, waving my hand in front of my face as a sickeningly sweet flowery smell suddenly filled the air.

Fink bent down and picked up the card.

"It's from Leslie," he groaned. "Why does she keep doing this?"

"I guess she's another leopard," I said.

"Yeah, well, this leopard's spots are going to have

to change, or I'm going to pull them off her with my bare hands," he said as he looked at the card.

"What did she do, spray that thing with her grandma's perfume?" I asked, still trying to wave the smell away.

"If you think it *smells* bad, check out what it *says*," he told me as he handed me the card. She'd drawn a big red heart and inside it, with a glitter pen, she'd written:

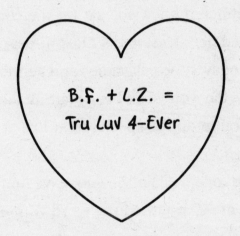

B.F. + L.Z. =
Tru Luv 4-Ever

Girls are so weird! I handed the card back to Fink. He took it, holding it at arm's distance by one corner, and walked over to Leslie Zebak's desk, where he dropped it like a dead fish in her lap.

"This stinks and so do you," he said. "Am I coming in loud and clear?"

She looked up at him with her big blue eyes, and instead of being insulted the way any normal person would have been, she giggled and blushed as though he'd just said something wonderful to her. I take back what I said before. Girls aren't weird, they're *beyond* weird.

When Mrs. West had taken attendance and collected the lunch money, she sat on the corner of her desk, crossed her arms, and smiled at us.

"Well, today's the day, ladies and gentlemen," she began. "The day you've all been waiting for. The day I finally let you in on the special treat I've been talking about."

I looked over at Fink, who gave me a double thumbs-up as he mouthed the word *Wash-ing-ton*.

"I had to keep you in suspense because there were a few details which needed to be worked out with the administration first," she told us. "But everything's been squared away now and I can finally tell you the big news."

The whole class was completely silent. We sat on the edge of our seats. I looked over at Fink again and he grinned at me.

"Some of you may have noticed posters and flyers around town for a group called Terpsichore Galore!" she said. "Has anybody heard of them?"

Nobody had.

"Does anyone know who Terpsichore is?" she asked.

Nobody did. Not even Jessie, who thinks she knows everything.

"Terpsichore is the Greek muse of dancing," Mrs. West told us. "Terpsichore Galore! is a modern dance troupe, headed by a brilliant woman named Tallulah Treehaven. I saw a performance several weeks ago and it gave me the most wonderful idea," she told us.

I didn't like the direction this was going in at all. What did modern dance have to do with a trip to Washington, D.C.? I shot a quick look at Fink. I could tell he was worried, too.

"After the performance I went backstage and asked Miss Treehaven if she would consider doing a dance project with our class," Mrs. West continued. "And guess what. She said yes! Isn't that exciting? We're all going to learn to dance!"

Washington, D.C., is exciting. Splash-o-Mania is exciting. Even cutting your toenails is exciting compared to learning how to dance. I didn't have to look over at Fink to know how he was taking the news. I was sure he was just as shocked and disappointed as I was.

"Starting today, every afternoon for the next two weeks, we'll be working with Tallulah Treehaven on a piece that she is going to personally choreograph especially for us," Mrs. West went on breathlessly. "Do you have any idea how lucky you are?"

Oh, yeah, I had a pretty good idea all right. Marla raised her hand.

"Yes, Miss Dundee," said Mrs. West.

"I've been taking ballet since I was three," Marla said proudly. "I'd be happy to help some of the others learn their steps. Of course, I'd be the only one allowed to wear toe shoes, since I'm so much more advanced than everyone else."

"Oh, please. You just got them yesterday, Marla," Jessie said.

"I'm sure Miss Treehaven will appreciate all the help she can get," Mrs. West said. "But as for the toe shoes, I don't think you'll be needing them. In modern dance, the dancers are usually barefoot or sometimes even in street shoes or sneakers."

"Will we have dance partners?" asked Leslie Zebak, turning around and flashing a big smile at Fink.

"I suppose it's possible," said Mrs. West. "We'll have to wait and see what Miss Treehaven has in mind. She'll be here this afternoon, right after lunch, so we'll hear all the details then."

"Are we going to give a performance when we're done?" asked Jessie.

"Oh, yes! Thank you for reminding me, Miss Kornblume," said Mrs. West. "If all goes well, at the end of the two weeks, we will indeed be putting on a performance for the entire school in the auditorium. It promises to be a wonderful event. Each and every one of you dancing onstage! Can you imagine?"

I could, but I didn't want to. I *really* didn't want to.

Dancing in front of the whole school! Even the squirty little kindergartners would be laughing at us. So much for Fink's theory that the bad thing wasn't going to be happening at school. As I reached down to scratch the red-hot fireball formerly known as my knee, Mad Dog shot another spit wad at me, this time missing completely and hitting Fink squarely on the ear.

"Ow!" he yelled.

"Is there a problem, Mr. Fink?" Mrs. West asked.

Fink shook his head. He knew better than to rat on Mad Dog. Making Mad Dog mad was like squirting a hose into a hornets' nest: You were bound to get stung, no matter how fast you ran in the other direction.

"No problem," he said, pulling the spitball out from behind his ear and flicking it onto the floor.

But there was a problem. Instead of going to Washington, D.C., some woman with a ridiculous name was planning to force us to dance in front of the whole school, and there wasn't anything we could do about it.

Or was there?

CHAPTER THREE

"No wonder you were itching," said Fink glumly, as we sat in the cafeteria together later that day eating lunch.

"I told you grown-ups have weird ideas about what's special," I said.

"Yeah, but *dance lessons*? That's not even close to being special," said Fink.

"I wish there was some way to get out of it," I said.

Fink's face lit up.

"Maybe there is!" he said. "For instance, we could volunteer to pull the curtains or hand out programs. Somebody's got to do those jobs, right?"

"Yeah. Why shouldn't it be us?" I asked.

"We better go back to class right now and ask Mrs. West before anybody else thinks of it," Fink said. "Come on, Nat-man. Let's go."

Fink shoved the last bite of his sandwich into his mouth and I gulped down what was left of my milk. We tossed out our trash and hurried back to the classroom to find Mrs. West.

When we got to the room, Mrs. West was there, but she was not alone. What appeared to be a large bird was perched on a tall stool next to her desk. It was covered with blue feathers and its feet were the brightest shade of orange I had ever seen in my life. We both stopped in our tracks and stared with our mouths hanging open.

"Where are your manners, gentlemen? Say hello to Miss Tallulah Treehaven," said Mrs. West.

Tallulah Treehaven wore a cape made of peacock feathers and, under it, a tight green shirt and a pair of bright orange tights. Her eyelids were painted the same remarkable shade of blue as the feathers, her lips were dark purply red, and on either side of her beaky nose a bright golden-brown eye struggled to stay open under the weight of the longest, heaviest fake eyelashes you could ever imagine. It looked like she'd glued two black tarantulas onto her eyes.

"Delighted, I'm sure," she said in a strange, throaty voice that sounded so funny, at first I thought she was joking.

But it was no joke. Tallulah Treehaven was real.

"Nat and I were wondering, Mrs. West, whether we could be the curtain pullers or the program hander-outers at the performance," Fink said as soon as he'd recovered from the sight of the bird lady.

"Nonsense," Talullah Treehaven said, jumping in before Mrs. West could even open her mouth to answer. "You will be dancers, not hander-outers."

"Trust me, Miss Treehaven, having Fink and me dance is a bad idea," I said.

"Not just bad," said Fink. "Dangerous."

"Yeah. You'd need to post a warning sign — Danger! Boys dancing!"

"Nonsense! When Tallulah says dance, everybody dances. Boys included," Miss Treehaven said, folding her wings — I mean arms — over her chest.

"But, Mrs. West, couldn't Nat and I just —" Fink started to say, but Mrs. West cut him off.

"You heard what Miss Treehaven said, Mr. Boyd," she told him firmly. "Everybody dances."

"But who's going to pull the curtain?" I asked desperately. "Someone's got to pull the curtain, don't they?"

"I can do it myself," said Mrs. West. "If Miss Treehaven says you dance, then you two are dancing and I don't want to hear another word about it!"

By then, other kids were coming into the room and it was obvious there was no point in arguing anymore. Mrs. West introduced everyone to Tallulah Treehaven, and then she told us to line up at the door.

"We'll be going to the gym for our first dance lesson," she explained.

Fink and I were the last to get in line. We were in no hurry to get to the gym.

"This is the first time in my whole life that I

haven't looked forward to going to the gym," I said
sadly.

"There has to be some way to get out of this,"
Fink said.

"Forget it, Fink," I said. "You heard what she said:
Everybody dances."

But Fink wasn't ready to give up.

"There has to be something we can do," he said.

"Dancing is an organic way to express human emotions," Miss Treehaven told us once we were all in the
gym.

I don't know about you, but when I hear *organic*, I
think granola, not dancing.

"It comes from the soul, the core," she went on.
"The body is merely the messenger. The message it-
self comes from within."

I didn't have any idea what Tallulah was talking
about, but I was perfectly happy to sit there listening.
At least we weren't dancing.

"Give me an emotion and I will demonstrate what
I mean," she said.

"How about joy?" suggested Mrs. West.

Without another word, Tallulah Treehaven began running around the gym, her feathered cape flying behind her. She leapt in the air, kicking her long orange legs and flapping her arms all over the place. I swear, it looked like any second she might actually take off and fly.

"Give me another!" she cried as she ran past us.

"Fear!" someone called out.

Suddenly, Tallulah Treehaven got down on her hands and knees and began crawling in circles around the floor, shaking and shivering and jerking her head backward over one shoulder as though she were being chased by something terrifying.

When she had finished, she stood up and peered out at us from under her eyelashes.

"There you have it," she said simply.

Mrs. West applauded appreciatively and some of the others — all girls, of course — clapped, too.

"Modern dance is about finding the emotion within and using the body to express it outwardly to the world," she explained breathlessly.

Apparently it was also about making a total fool of yourself in front of a roomful of people.

"Now, boys and girls, we shall go in search of your inner selves," she told us.

At first, nobody moved. But then Marla, the big show-off, got up and started dancing all fancy up on her toes.

"*Faboo!*" cried Miss Treehaven.

"I've been taking ballet since I was three," Marla called out to her. "I'm advanced — watch this!"

She started spinning around on her toes.

"Lovely!" Miss Treehaven said.

Then, all of a sudden, a deep voice came from the back of the room. "That's nothing. Check this out."

Miss Treehaven didn't know enough to be afraid, but we all knew who that voice belonged to. Everyone moved out of the way as Mad Dog stood up, spread his huge arms wide and started spinning, too.

Marla stopped long enough to see that he was trying to steal the spotlight from her. Her beady little eyes narrowed into two angry slits and she began to spin again, this time even faster. Pretty soon the two of them were spinning so fast they were nothing but blurs.

We all saw what was coming.

"Watch out!" cried Mrs. West and Miss Treehaven at the same time.

But it was too late. Mad Dog and Marla collided with a sickening *thunk* and fell in a heap on the gym floor, their arms and legs hopelessly tangled together. Mad Dog started laughing, but Marla was furious.

"If you've injured any of my limbs, my father is going to sue you, you hideous slug!" Marla screamed. "You apologize right now! Do you hear me? Right now!"

"Me? Why should I apologize?" asked Mad Dog, pushing her off him and standing up. "I was just doing what the lady said, finding my inner self. I can't help it if you're so clumsy you ran right into me."

"*Clumsy?*" Marla screamed. "I take ballet!"

"Yeah? Well, you better take some more 'cause your dancing stinks," said Mad Dog.

Together, Mrs. West and Miss Treehaven helped

Marla to stand up. Her hair was kind of messed up, but otherwise she seemed to be okay.

"Perhaps in the future we can all take a lesson from Miss Dundee and Mr. Ditmeyer and remember to keep some distance between ourselves when we are dancing," suggested Mrs. West.

"A mile away sounds about right when it comes to her," muttered Mad Dog, jerking his head toward Marla.

"Everybody up!" shouted Miss Treehaven, gesturing for us all to stand. "Boys, too! The time has come!"

"Time to go back to class?" I asked hopefully, as I stood up.

No such luck. She meant the time had come for all of us, including Fink and me, to get out on the dance floor and express our inner selves. For sixty excruciating minutes, Miss Treehaven made us practice what she called "moving moments." Each horrifying moment seemed to last an eternity. We had to curl up into little balls then slowly unwind and "blossom" into flowers. We had to sway like giant redwoods with our arms up over our heads and wiggle around on the floor pretending to be rushing mountain brooks. I looked over at Fink at one point and I could tell he was thinking the same thing I was — *Help!*

When it was over, Mrs. West made a little speech about how honored we were to be working with Miss Treehaven, and how could we ever repay her, and all sorts of other grateful junk like that. Then we had to line up single file so we could walk past Miss Treehaven, shake hands with her, and thank her personally for the wonderful experience.

On the way back to class, Fink left his place in line to come up and walk next to me.

"I have never been so humiliated in my entire life," he said. "And that includes the time my bathing suit fell off when I dove into the pool last summer."

"Tell me about it," I said. "It was bad enough today. What's it going to be like when we have to do it onstage in front of an *audience*?"

"We're not going to let that happen," said Fink.

"How are we going to stop it?" I asked.

"Don't worry — I'll think of something," he told me.

That afternoon after school, we were sitting up in our tree again, talking.

"What do you think would happen if we lay down on the floor and refused to get up until Mrs. West promises that we don't have to dance?" he asked me.

"What do I think would happen? I think Mrs. West would have a fit," I answered, "especially if we did it in front of a guest."

"Why does she think Beulah Bushheaven is such a big deal?" Fink asked. "Whoever heard of her, anyway?"

"Her name is *Treehaven*," I corrected him. "Talullah Treehaven."

"Whatever," said Fink. "The point is, Mrs. West thinks she's great, but we don't. Because of her, instead of going to Washington, D.C., we're going to have to put on tights and jump around like fools in front of the whole school."

"Wait a second," I said. "Who said anything about wearing tights?"

"She was wearing them today, wasn't she?" Fink pointed out.

"That doesn't necessarily mean we're going to have to, does it?" I asked.

"Let's put it this way," said Fink. "I think it means there's a pretty good chance we will."

I didn't say anything. I was too busy scratching my suddenly very itchy knee.

CHAPTER FOUR

On the way to school the next morning we saw the Red Devils up ahead of us. Their red hair was pulled back into ponytails, which swung back and forth in rhythm as they walked. As usual, they were dressed in matching outfits — yellow pants and white sweatshirts with sparkling rainbows on the backs. To my surprise, as soon as we saw them, Fink started running toward them calling their names.

"Marla! Jessie! Hey, you guys! Wait up!" he yelled.

"What are you doing?" I said, grabbing hold and yanking his arm to try to stop him.

Too late. The girls stopped and waited for us on the corner.

"What do you want?" Jessie asked when we caught up with them.

"Yeah, what do you want?" echoed Marla, tapping her foot impatiently. "We don't want to be late for school."

"We just want to talk to you for a minute," said Fink.

"We do?" I asked, surprised.

"Yes. We want your expert opinion on something," Fink told them.

"What are you talking about?" asked Jessie.

"Yeah, what are you talking about?" Marla and I said at the exact same time.

Without thinking, because it's a habit with Fink and me, I said, "Jinx on Froozles!" and punched Marla in the arm.

"Ouch!" she yelled, rubbing her arm. "Nat Boyd, I'm warning you. If that leaves a bruise on me —"

"I know, I know. Your father is going to sue me," I finished her sentence for her.

"I've had it with you boys. You're all so violent," Marla said.

"Calm down," Fink said. "He didn't punch you that hard. And besides, he didn't mean anything by it. It's just a game we play."

"You boys and your silly little games," sniffed Jessie. "Why did you want us to wait for you? So you could punch us like a couple of barbarians?"

"First of all, nobody punched *you*, Corn Bloomers," Fink said. "And second of all, like I told you, we just want to talk to you for a minute. Is that so barbaric?"

"That depends. What do you want to talk to us about?" Jessie asked, her eyes narrowing with suspicion behind her glasses.

"Dancing," Fink said.

Both girls seemed surprised, and frankly, so was I. Marla took a step forward and expertly flipped her red hair over her shoulders.

"*I'm* the more advanced dancer, so you should ask me," she said.

I saw Jessie roll her eyes. Even she has trouble taking Marla sometimes, and they're best friends!

"Go ahead, ask the big expert," Jessie said with a wave of her hand.

"What do you want to know?" Marla asked, clearly pleased to be the center of attention all of a sudden.

"We want to know what modern dance is," Fink said, "and more importantly, we want to know whether the boys have to wear tights when they do it."

"Go ahead, Marla, *tell them*," said Jessie.

"Okay. Modern dance is, well, it's *modern*," Marla began, "and ballet is, well, it's *classical*, which means historically —"

"They're not interested in the history of ballet," Jessie interrupted impatiently. "All they want to know is whether or not they're going to have to wear tights. Right, Boyds?"

She looked at Fink and me, and we both nodded.

"Tell them, Marla. *Tell them about the tights*," Jessie said.

Marla looked confused, as if she wasn't quite sure what she was supposed to say, so Jessie took over.

"I guess Marla doesn't want to be the one to give you the bad news," she said, turning to us with a serious look on her face. "Because the answer is *yes*, you do have to wear tights. All the boys do."

"Are you sure?" Fink asked.

"Positive," said Jessie.

"Positive," Marla echoed. "The boys always have to wear tights when they do modern dance. Oh, and in case you're wondering, usually they're flesh-colored."

"Which in your case would mean pink," Jessie pointed out.

"*What?*" said Fink. "Pink tights?"

Both girls nodded.

"They'll also have to wear pink leotards, right, Marla?" said Jessie.

"Yep. They're very tight, too. That way, from far away you look like you're naked," she explained. "That's an important part of modern dance; the boys are always supposed to look naked."

Fink and I were speechless.

"If you're lucky, maybe Miss Treehaven will let you wear tutus like the girls do," Jessie said. "At least they cover you up a little."

"What the heck is a tutu?" I asked.

"It's a fluffy little skirt that sticks out all the way around your middle," Marla explained.

"Pink, of course," added Jessie.

"I have one if you want to borrow it so you can get used to how it feels to dance in one," Marla offered.

Fink and I were speechless again. *Pink tights and skirts?*

"Anything else you want to know?" Marla asked.

We both shook our heads. We'd heard more than enough already.

"Okay then, we'd better get going or we'll be late," said Jessie. "Glad we could help answer your questions."

"If you change your minds about borrowing the tutu, just let me know," Marla called to us over her shoulder as the two of them walked away, ponytails swinging in sync again.

We let them get far enough ahead of us so that we could walk and talk without them overhearing us.

"What are we going to do, Fink?" I asked. "Pink tights and skirts."

"I know," he said. "I heard."

In all the years I've known him, Fink has never let me down. No matter how bad things get, he always manages to come up with a plan for how to make things better. But as we walked in silence the rest of the way to school, I knew we were both worried. What if there was no way out of it?

All morning long, the girls kept talking about how they couldn't wait for the afternoon to come so they could work with Miss Treehaven again. Fink and I, of course, were dreading it, and we weren't the only ones. All the boys were grumbling about how embarrassing it had been the day before.

"Mrs. West, can we invite our parents to the dance performance, too?" Leslie Zebak asked at one point.

"I could stay after school today and design an invitation," offered Bethany Jenkins, the best artist in our class. "Maybe something with dancing butterflies on it."

"What a lovely idea!" said Mrs. West. "Yes, let's do invite the parents."

Oh, great. Now we were going to have to dance in front of the whole school *and* our parents.

At lunch, Fink and I ate together at our usual table.

"Haven't you come up with anything yet?" I asked.

"I'm working on it, Nat-o," he said.

"Well, hurry up, will you?" I said, looking up at the big clock on the wall. "Lunch is over in twenty minutes, and my inner self doesn't feel like getting expressed again today."

Our moment of despair was suddenly interrupted by a loud *bang!* We both nearly jumped out of our skins.

"What was that?" I yelled.

We dove under the table.

It was only Mad Dog. He'd snuck up behind us, blown air into his brown paper lunch bag, and popped it right behind our heads. He was laughing.

"Since you're already down there on the ground, why don't you two ballerinas act like a couple of seeds and sprout," said Mad Dog.

"Have a heart, Mad Dog, will you?" I groaned, crawling out from under the table. "We're freaking out here just fine without any help from you."

Mad Dog just kept laughing, his shiny silver braces,

my mother's handiwork, glinting in the sunlight that streamed through the lunchroom windows.

"Go ahead and laugh all you want, Mad Dog, because you're not going to be laughing anymore when you have to go out onstage in front of everybody wearing pink tights," said Fink, as he brushed himself off and sat back down in his chair.

Mad Dog stopped laughing and grabbed Fink's sleeve.

"What are you talking about, Finky boy?" he growled. "I'm not wearing tights."

"Yes, you are," said Fink. "We all have to wear them."

"Oh, yeah? And who's gonna make me, huh?" said Mad Dog as he balled up his fist and looked like he was getting ready to take a swing at Fink.

"Beulah Bushheaven, that's who," said Fink.

"Tallulah Treehaven," I corrected.

"No way am I putting on tights!" said Mad Dog.

"Yes, you are. You're wearing tights and so are we. All the boys have to," Fink told him again.

David Framer and Danny Lebson, who happened to be walking by at that moment, stopped to listen.

"Who's wearing tights?" asked David.

"Not me," said Mad Dog. "And anybody who thinks I am has got another think coming."

A couple more boys walked over and joined us.

"What's going on?" they asked.

"Fink is going to make Mad Dog wear tights," Danny Lebson explained.

"*I'm* not the one who's going to make him wear tights," Fink said. "Beulah Bushheaven is."

"It's Treehaven, Fink," I told him again. "Tallulah Treehaven."

But Fink ignored me and went on.

"At the performance, the boys are going to have to wear flesh-colored tights and these leotard things that make you look like you don't have any clothes on at all," Fink told the gathering crowd of boys.

"Get out," whispered Danny, his eyes wide as silver dollars.

"Are you sure?" asked David.

"Absolutely," said Fink solemnly, "and if we're *lucky*, we might get to wear tutus."

"What's a tutu?" asked Mad Dog. There was something in his voice I'd never heard before. *Fear.*

"Some kind of a skirt," I told him.

Everyone gasped.

"We have to do something," said Fink.

There were murmurs of agreement from the crowd.

"We have to band together," Fink went on. "We have to let them know we're not going to take this!"

More murmurs from the crowd.

"What are we going to do?" someone asked.

I guess everybody rallying together like that finally gave Fink the inspiration he needed.

"I've got a plan. I'm calling an emergency meeting of all the boys in our class right after school," said Fink. "We'll meet out in the yard under the last basketball hoop on the left and I'll fill you in."

"What if Mrs. West sees us?" asked Danny nervously.

"If you can't stand the heat, get out of the kitchen," I said, before I could stop myself.

Everyone turned and looked at me funny. Luckily the bell rang and we all started back to class.

"Remember, right after school under the last basketball hoop," Fink reminded us as we made our way out into the hall. "Be there, or be square."

This time it was my turn to look at him funny.

"Where did that come from?" I asked. "I've never heard you say that before."

"Hey, you're not the only one who's allowed to use expressions around here, you know," he said.

"Hey, Fink," said Danny Lebson, joining us as we walked up the steps of the school. "Can't you tell us the plan right now, so we don't have to dance again this afternoon?"

"There isn't time," Fink said. "We're just going to have to grit our teeth and get through it today. But have no fear, tomorrow we show Beulah Bushheaven that the men of 6-W are not a bunch of tutu-wearing, naked-looking wimps," Fink said, pounding his fist into his palm for emphasis.

This time I didn't bother to correct Fink. Why should I care if he said her name wrong? If Tallulah

Treehaven wasn't stopped, every boy in our class was going to be humiliated in front of the whole school — not to mention our parents. And everybody knows parents are experts at catching your most embarrassing moments on film so that you can relive them over and over again for the rest of your life.

Fink needed to focus on one thing and one thing only — leading us into battle against the thing every boy dreads more than bee stings, brussel sprouts, and booster shots combined — *dancing*.

CHAPTER FIVE

The second session with Miss Treehaven wasn't as bad as the first. It was *worse*.

"Human mirrors," Miss Treehaven told us, "is a *faboo* exercise for getting in touch with your own body. It's important to do this with someone the right size, though, so please look around the room and choose a partner approximately the same height as yourself."

Fink and I are not the same height. I'm a lot taller than he is, but we didn't care what Miss Treehaven said. We wanted to be partners anyway.

"Mr. Fink," Mrs. West said, coming over to where Fink and I were standing, "although I know you enjoy

Mr. Boyd's company immensely, I'm afraid you two don't make suitable partners."

She looked around the room.

"How about me?" asked Leslie Zebak, raising her hand. "I'm the same size as Boyd."

Fink looked horrified as Mrs. West brought Leslie over to stand next to him.

"Perfect," she said, measuring them back to back. "Now all we need to do is find a good partner for you, Mr. Boyd."

Mrs. West shifted a few people around until she was finally satisfied that she'd found us all the right partners. Jeremy Huan was with David Framer, Marla was with Bethany. At first I thought I was going to end up being with Jessie, but at the last minute Mrs. West decided to put her with Danny Lebson and that left only one person to be my partner. Mad Dog.

"Well, it's not a perfect match," she said, standing us back to back, "but it will have to do."

Not a perfect match? That was the understatement of the century! Mad Dog looked at me and growled.

"The object of this exercise is to do exactly what your partner does," Miss Treehaven explained, "as though you were each standing in front of a mirror. If she raises her right hand, you mirror her by raising your left. If he tilts his head left, you tilt yours right. Understand?"

I understood all right, but I wasn't sure I could do it. Generally speaking, I make an effort to stay as far away from Mad Dog as possible. Being right up close to him like that was making my palms sweat.

"Begin!" cried Miss Treehaven.

I looked at Mad Dog, who growled again, raised his right fist, and shook it at me. Remembering what Miss Treehaven had said, I did the opposite of what he was doing. I raised my left fist and shook it at him.

I guess Mad Dog hadn't been listening to the instructions, because he took it the wrong way and grabbed my fist, forcing me down onto my knees.

"Beg for mercy, ballerina boy!" he shouted.

"Mercy!" I yelled as Mad Dog twisted my wrist. "Mercy, mercy, mercy!"

"No physical contact, boys!" cried Miss Treehaven

over the yelling. "You are not interacting, you are mir-roring."

Mad Dog let go of me and I stood up. My knees were shaking and my wrist was slightly numb.

"Try again," Miss Treehaven said, coming over and standing next to us.

I decided it would be safer if I took the lead, so I raised my good hand at him, waved and smiled. At least he couldn't misinterpret that.

"Now you raise your left hand and wave back at him," Miss Treehaven instructed Mad Dog. "Make the movements match."

It was hard to keep smiling and waving, knowing that at any second that wave from Mad Dog's big paw could turn into a smack, but I did the best I could.

"Much better," said Miss Treehaven.

My arm was tired, so I changed the movement and turned my head to the right. Mad Dog looked left. I looked up, and Mad Dog looked up. Then I turned left — and my mouth fell open. I couldn't be-lieve what I saw! Poor Fink. Leslie Zebak was leaning toward him, just inches away from his face with her eyes closed and her mouth all puckered up like she was going to kiss him.

"No way!" he shouted, stomping his foot. "I'm not doing this anymore. It's sick!"

"Mr. Fink!" Mrs. West said sternly. "You're disrupting the exercise."

"But she's making smoochy faces at me," said Fink.

Everybody laughed and Fink's face turned really red.

"Fink and Zebak, sitting in a tree, k-i-s-s-i-n-g," taunted Mad Dog.

"Knock it off, Mad Dog," I whispered. "Remember he's the one who's got the plan for keeping you out of pink tights."

"Oh, yeah, I forgot," he said.

Fortunately, Miss Treehaven decided we'd done enough mirroring for one day and told us to stop. For the rest of the hour, we practiced leaping, which was awful, but at least it didn't involve having to look at Mad Dog up close.

*   *   *

All the boys from Mrs. West's class met after school that afternoon, out in the yard under the last basketball hoop on the left.

"Is everybody here?" asked Fink, looking around.

"Everybody but Henry. He was absent today, the lucky duck," somebody said.

"Somebody can call him later and fill him in," said Fink. "We're going to need one hundred percent participation for this plan to work."

"Do you really have a plan?" asked Danny Lebson.

"Of course I do," said Fink.

We all gathered around close as Fink laid out his plan for us.

"Here's what we do. Tomorrow morning, everybody make sure to bring a bag lunch from home, with a tuna fish sandwich in it. Okay? Then, exactly a half hour after lunch, we all pretend that we got food poisoning from a bad batch of tuna. If you've ever had food poisoning, then you know there's absolutely no way you could possibly dance when you're that sick," Fink said.

Danny tentatively raised his hand.

53

"I'm allergic to tuna fish," he said. "My mom doesn't even have it in the house. She always packs turkey and cheese for me."

"So pretend you got your sandwich mixed up with somebody else's, and instead of food poisoning, you can fake an allergic reaction," Fink told him.

I know that best friends are supposed to support each other, but I felt I had to point out the giant hole in Fink's plan.

"Maybe we can pull that off for tomorrow, but what are we going to do the next day? Get food poisoning all over again from something else?" I asked.

"Yeah, Nat's right," somebody said. "We've got two weeks of dance classes to get out of, plus the performance. We can't get food poisoning that many times, can we?"

"Your plan stinks," grumbled Mad Dog.

"I'd like to see you come up with something better," said Fink.

"I'd like to see you make me," said Mad Dog, puffing his chest out and taking a menacing step toward Fink.

"Hold on," I said quickly. "We can't afford to argue right now. We have to stick together. Does anybody have any other ideas besides us getting food poisoning?"

"We could all pretend to be sick tomorrow and just not show up," someone suggested.

"That has the same problem as the food-poisoning idea," I said.

"My mom told me that in the 1960s, people used to chain themselves to things to protest the war. Maybe we should chain ourselves to something," suggested Jeremy Huan. "Like our desks, for instance."

A few people thought that might be a good idea until Jeremy went on to explain that his mother had also told him that those people usually ended up getting arrested and taken off to jail.

"I say we kidnap the bird lady and put her in a cage. We could charge five bucks for people to come see her dance in there," said Mad Dog.

Yep, it really doesn't take much of a stretch of the imagination to see Mad Dog ending up throwing rocks at squirrels when he grows up.

Fink had wandered off to the side of the crowd while all of this was going on. I thought maybe he was mad because I'd shot down his food-poisoning idea. But suddenly he raised both arms in the air and shouted, "Eureka! I've got it!"

Everyone gathered around him again.

"Does anybody remember what Mrs. West said about the performance we're going to be putting on at the end of this thing?" he asked.

"She said the whole school was going to come," said David.

"Plus our families," added Jeremy.

"And she said we're all going to have to be in it," I said.

"Yeah, but does anybody remember *exactly* what she said?" asked Fink, looking around.

Nobody did.

"She said, 'If all goes well, we're going to put on a performance,'" said Fink.

"So?" I said.

"Don't you get it?" he asked. "She said *if all goes*

well. That's it! That's the answer! If we want to get out of having to perform, all we have to do is make sure that all does *not* go well."

"How are we going to do that?" somebody asked.

"Without getting in trouble with Mrs. West?" asked somebody else.

"We have to be bad," said Fink.

"That should be easy," said Mad Dog. "I'm an expert in that department."

"Not that kind of bad," said Fink. "I mean we have to be bad at dancing."

"We were all bad at dancing on the very first day," I said. "And that didn't stop us from having to dance again today."

"That's because we weren't bad enough," Fink said.

"How bad do we have to be?" I asked.

"Really bad," said Fink. "I'm telling you, if we totally stink, this will work. *She won't want us to dance.*"

We all stood there for a minute letting Fink's plan soak in.

"It's way better than the tuna fish idea," said Danny finally.

"So are you guys with me?" asked Fink.

Tallulah Treehaven may have thought she'd seen bad dancing before, but she hadn't seen anything yet. The boys of 6-W had a plan, and nothing was going to stop us now!

CHAPTER SIX

After our meeting broke up, Fink and I walked over to the Bee Hive.

"Want a Froozle?" he asked me.

"No, thanks," I said. "You know my mom won't let me have those. Too much sugar."

"There's no such thing as too much sugar," said Fink.

I probably should have offered to pay for Fink's Froozle since I owed him twenty-seven of them, but my mom had given me my allowance the night be-fore, and I finally had enough to pay for my rat.

"Want to go to Purr-fect Pets with me after this

and pick out my rat?" I asked Fink, as he peeled the paper off a straw and took a long drink of his Froozle.

"I don't know," he said. "I've got a clarinet lesson on Saturday, and I should probably go home and practice."

"Can't you practice later?" I asked. "I really want you to come with me. I have to make sure I pick the best rat."

After I bugged him a little more, Fink finally agreed to come with me to the pet store. He finished up his Froozle as we walked.

"You're sure you want a rat, not a newt, right?" he asked me.

"Yeah. They're supposed to be very smart," I said.

"How about a pig? Pigs are supposed to be very smart, too," he said. "And they don't have hair either."

"Yes, they do," I said.

"Pigs? They don't have hair. They're bald, like newts," Fink said.

"No, they're not. They have hair," I said.

"Pink hair?" said Fink. "I don't think so."

"Haven't you ever seen a pig up close?" I asked. "Trust me — they have hair."

"Is it pink?" Fink said.

"No, the skin underneath is pink. The hair is kind of whitish and thin, so the skin shows through," I said.

"Oh, kind of like my Uncle Barry. His skin used to show through, too, before he got his rug," said Fink.

"His rug?" I asked.

"Yeah, you know, his toupee. It's made out of real hair. Actually, it's my Aunt Jane's hair. She got her hair cut short, and afterward she asked the barber to put everything he'd chopped off in a bag for her so she could take it to this wig maker she knows. Now she and Uncle Barry have the same hair, only he takes his off at night and sets it on top of the lampshade so the dog won't chew on it," Fink told me.

"Too much information, Fink," I said. "Way too much."

When we got to Purr-fect Pets, Fink started to push open the door, but suddenly he stopped.

"Quick! Run for your life!" he said, grabbing my elbow and trying to pull me down the sidewalk.

"Wait a second! Let go of me, will you? I want to go in and get my rat," I said as I tried to shake him loose.

"Trust me, you don't want to go in there. There's something dangerous inside," Fink said, and he started pulling me down the street.

"What are you talking about?" I asked.

But before he could answer, the dangerous thing Fink was talking about pushed open the door and came charging down the street after us.

It was Leslie Zebak.

"Wait!" she cried as she ran after us. "Where are you guys going?"

"Run!" said Fink.

"No!" I told him. "Come on, Fink, I want to get my rat today. Who cares if she's there, too?"

"I care," said Fink.

"Then think of some way to get rid of her," I said.

Leslie had caught up with us and was standing there smiling at Fink.

"Hello, Boyd," she said in a sweet voice. "I was hoping we might run into each other."

"Gee, that's funny, Leslie. I was hoping we wouldn't," answered Fink.

Leslie was holding a large bag of rabbit food she'd just bought.

"I had to come pick up some food for Mr. Nibbles. It sure is heavy. Maybe you could help me carry it home," she said.

"Sorry, I'm busy," said Fink, as he walked past her and pushed open the door of the store. I followed him in and we headed to the back of the store where the rats and mice are kept. Leslie came, too.

"What are you doing here, anyway?" asked Leslie. "Do you have a pet, too?"

Fink stopped walking and it was clear that the wheels were turning in his head. I knew he wanted to get rid of her, and I wondered how he planned to do it.

"We're here to look at the *rats*," he said. "Do you like *rats*, Leslie?"

So that was it. He was trying to scare Leslie away by talking about rats. I guess he figured that most girls were afraid of rats, but that was not the case with Leslie Zebak.

"I *love* rats," she said. "We used to have one for a pet. He had the cutest little pink eyes, but a couple of months ago he got sick and died. That's when we got Mr. Nibbles."

"How about *snakes*?" asked Fink, obviously not ready to give up on his plan yet. "Do you like those?"

"No," said Leslie with a shudder. "I hate snakes."

Score!

"Oh, too bad, because I'm here to buy one," he told her. "I was thinking about maybe getting a python or a boa constrictor. Something really big and fat around the middle, you know?"

"Ugh," said Leslie with another shudder. "I thought you said you were here to look at rats."

"We are. Rat babies — you know, pinkies," Fink told her.

"Pinkies?" she asked softly.

"Yeah, defenseless little baby rats. That's what snakes eat. It's kind of like popcorn to them. They just pop 'em in their mouths, and down the hatch they go!"

Leslie turned pale and she blinked her eyes a few times really fast.

"Want to watch me feed some pinkies to the snakes?" Fink asked.

"Uh, no, thanks. I think I'd better get that food home to Mr. Nibbles," she said. "Right away."

As the door closed behind Leslie, Fink broke into a huge grin.

"Wow," I said. "That was impressive."

"Did you see the look on her face when I told her about the pinkies?" he laughed. "Now let's go pick out your rat so I can get home and practice my clarinet before my mom blows up."

Choosing the right rat proved to be a lot harder than I expected. I didn't want my rat to be a sleepy one, because it would be kind of boring if all it did was lie around napping all day. On the other hand, I didn't want it to be too hyper, either, because then it might be hard to catch when I wanted to hold and play with it.

"What do you think about that cute little one over there?" I asked, pointing to a smallish rat sitting in the corner of the cage nibbling on a kernel of dried corn it was holding in its front paws.

"Look, Nat-o, no offense or anything," said Fink, "but these bald rats all look the same to me, and frankly, none of them are exactly what you'd call cute. They look like big pink baked potatoes, only squishy. Are you sure you want one of these? They're kind of gross."

"No, they're not. They're cool. You're just not used to the way they look yet. I've been checking them out on the Internet for months," I told him. "They grow on you."

"Okay, if you say so. Can we just pick one and get out of here, please? They're creeping me out with those pink eyes and see-through ears. Ugh," said Fink.

"I want to get the right one," I explained. "They all have different personalities."

"Rat-alities, you mean," he said.

"Some are smarter than others," I said. "I definitely want mine to be smart."

"How are you going to tell which one is the smartest, give them an IQ test?" asked Fink. "Come on, Natalie, I have to get home or my mom is going to make me practice double."

"I can't decide," I said. "It's between that one in the corner eating the corn and the big one with the long whiskers."

"Go with the big one," said Fink.

"You think?" I said. "The other one has a little notch in one ear and it *looks* smart. See what I mean? Look at the intelligence in those eyes."

"Okay, fine. Go with the corn eater if you think it's such a genius," said Fink. "Just pick one already."

The pet store manager came over to us at that point.

"You boys planning on buying a Sphinx?" he asked.

"A what?" asked Fink.

"A Sphinx," said the manager. "That's what the true hairless rats are called."

"I'm planning to buy one," I said. "I've got it narrowed down to two and I'm just trying to make up my mind."

"Before you decide, do you mind if I ask you a couple of questions?" he asked. "A pet, even if it's a small one, is a big responsibility. Are your parents aware that you're planning to purchase a rat?" he asked.

"Oh, yeah. His mom knows all about it. He's been saving his allowance for weeks to get the ten bucks," said Fink. "She may not be so happy about it when she sees how ugly they are, though."

"They're not ugly!" the manager and I said at exactly the same time. This time, I resisted my natural instinct to punch him in the arm and yell, "Jinx on Froozles!"

"So you've saved up ten dollars, huh?" said the manager. "That's a good start. It's enough to cover the cost of the animal, but you know you're going to a need a few other things, too."

"Like what?" I asked.

"For starters, you're going to need a cage, bedding material, food, a water bottle, a food dish, and if you want your rat to be happy, you'll want to consider an exercise wheel as well," he said, ticking things off on his fingers as he spoke.

My heart sank. I hadn't thought about any of that. I had four weeks' allowance saved up. Twelve dollars. That was it. I'd figured that would cover the cost of the rat plus tax, and I'd have enough money left over to put a little bit back in my piggy bank so it wouldn't be completely empty.

"How much is all that stuff going to cost?" asked Fink.

"Somewhere in the neighborhood of fifty dollars, depending on whether you go with a metal cage or a glass aquarium," he said.

"*Fifty dollars?*" I said. I did the math in my head. Three into fifty, one carry the two . . . it would take me more than four months to save that much more! And that was only if I didn't spend a cent on anything else. No movies, no baseball cards, no nothing.

"I might be able to knock a few bucks off the price if you're willing to take a tank with a slight crack in it," said the manager.

I looked at the rat sitting in the corner of the cage — the small one with the notched ear. It had finished the corn and was washing its whiskers. Suddenly it stopped and looked right at me and in that instant I knew that was the one I wanted. That was my rat.

"Could I show you something a little less expensive? We've got a special going on newts this week," the manager suggested.

"Yeah, Nat-o. How about a newt?" said Fink. "I'm telling you, they're very cool."

I shook my head sadly.

"Let's just go," I said.

"You're sure you don't want to take a look at those newts?" asked the manager. "I could toss in some mealyworms, no charge."

"No, thanks," I said, as I pulled open the door.

On the way home, Fink and I didn't talk much. What was there to say, really? What a crummy week it had been. I'd been promised a trip to Washington, D.C., which turned out to be dance lessons, then Mad

Dog had almost broken my wrist, and now, on top of all of that, I'd lost my rat.

"Maybe some relative will send you money for your birthday," said Fink.

"My birthday is months away. By the time I save enough money, the rat I want won't be there anymore. It's the cutest one. Somebody's going to buy it for sure," I said.

"Maybe not," said Fink. "Not everyone thinks they're quite as cute as you do, Nat-o."

Fink and I live on the same street, just a few houses away from each other. When we turned up our block, he reached over and patted me on the back.

"Don't worry, Nat-man. I'll figure out a way to get you that rat," he said. "In fact, I've already got an idea of how to do it."

Where was Fink going to get the money? I tried to feel hopeful, but I couldn't — not with the way my luck had been going lately. I might as well just kiss that perfect rat good-bye. It was just not meant to be.

CHAPTER SEVEN

My mom was in the kitchen making dinner when I got home. I smelled onions frying and hoped she was making her special spaghetti sauce. It has onions in it and it's one of my favorites.

"Where's your rat?" she asked me. "I thought you said you were getting it today."

I shrugged. I didn't feel like telling her the whole sad story.

"What's for dinner?" I asked, changing the subject.

"Liver and onions," she said.

Of course it would be liver and onions. I *hate* liver and onions. It couldn't be spaghetti. That would be *good*, and nothing *good* was allowed to happen to me because I was the unluckiest kid in Jeffersonville.

"I'm going upstairs to lie down for a while," I said.

"You're not feeling sick, are you, sweetie?" my mom asked, drying her hands on a towel and then pressing one cool palm against my forehead to see if I had a fever.

"I'm fine," I said, pushing her hand away and heading upstairs to my room. "I'm just tired, that's all."

I figured if I lay down and took a nap, at least I could escape from the reality of my unlucky life for a little while.

Yeah, right. What was I thinking? When *lucky* people go to sleep they have sweet dreams. Me? I had a nightmare.

It started out okay. I was walking down the street, drinking a cherry Froozle. That's how I could tell I was dreaming. The only place I would ever be allowed to have one of those would be in my dreams. Anyway, there I was, walking along, minding my own business, when suddenly Marla Dundee shows up pulling a little wagon behind her with a big box in it.

"What's in the box?" I ask her.

"Wouldn't *you* like to know?" Marla said.

"Yeah. I would like to know. That's why I asked you what's in the box," I said. My dreams are always very realistic when it comes to the way people talk to each other.

So Marla tells me to go ahead and open the box if I'm so curious, and that's when the nightmare part begins. The minute I pull open the cardboard flaps, Jessie Kornblume jumps out of the box! Her red hair is all piled up fancy and there is a wreath of flowers around her head. I don't even have to look to know what she's wearing. Jessie shows up in a lot of my nightmares, and for some reason she's always wearing the same thing — a big, poofy, white wedding dress. Talk about scary! Sometimes that's all it takes — seeing her in that dress — to make me wake up. But this time there's more. Instead of a bouquet, which is what brides usually hold in their hands, Jessie's holding a rat. Not just any rat — a hairless rat. *My* hairless rat. The one with the notched ear.

"Hey, where did you get that?" I ask her.

"I bought it," she says.

"But that's *my* rat!" I tell her.

"No, it's not. It's *my* rat," she says. "I bought it with my own money. Marla and I are going to teach it how to dance. They're very smart, you know." And then she gets this sneaky look in her beady little eyes. "You wish this rat was yours, don't you?" she asks.

"It *is* mine," I say. "I picked it out. I just didn't have enough money to buy all the stuff for it. Do you have all the stuff for it?"

"Uh-huh. It's got a cage and a wheel, and we even made it a little pink tutu," she says. "For when we teach it how to dance."

"Oh, please," I say, getting down on my knees in front of her, "please give me my rat!"

"You want me to give you this rat?" she asks.

"Yes! I do!" I cry. "I do!"

"No, no, no," she says, wagging her finger at me. "I'm not going to give it to you. But there *is* another way for this rat to be yours."

"What do I have to do?" I ask. "Just tell me. I'll do anything."

"Marry me!" she exclaims.

"Marry you?" I ask.

"Yes. If we're married, then the rat will belong to us both. It will be *our* rat, till death do us part. Look! You're already down on your knees. All you have to do is ask me to marry you and the rat will be yours."

Then she puckers up her lips and leans down like she's going to kiss me and that's when the first piece of good luck I'd had in a long time happened. I woke up.

The smell of frying liver filled the air. Sometimes life really stinks. Liver and onions, or marrying Jessie? What a choice. It was like an A or B Fink and I might have come up with. I chose the slightly less disgusting of the two things, got up, washed my face and hands, and went downstairs to dinner.

"I saw Mrs. Dundee at the supermarket this afternoon, and she told me that there's going to be a dance performance at your school next week," my mother said as she served up my plate and passed it to me. "How come I haven't heard anything about this?"

"I think maybe it's going to get canceled," I said.

"Really? What a shame. I could have taped it with my new video camera," my mother said.

Parents are so predictable sometimes.

The next morning at school the boys in our class were all very nervous. Fink kept looking at the clock. I knew he felt responsible. After all, he was the one who'd thought up the plan. If it didn't work, everyone would blame him.

Boys kept coming over to Fink with questions.

"The plan is still on, right?" whispered Danny.

"How will we know if we're being bad enough?" asked Jeremy.

Fink kept telling them not to worry, that he would start the ball rolling and we'd know what to do when the time came.

"Do you really think it's going to work?" I asked, as we stood in line in the hall waiting for a turn at the drinking fountain.

"Absolutely," he said. "She's no match for us."

There was that famous Fink confidence.

"I hope you're right," I said. "But I have my doubts."

"What's the matter with you today?" Fink asked. "You seem weird."

"I'm in a bad mood," I told him. "I can't stop thinking about that rat."

"Don't worry about the rat," Fink said. "I told you, I'm already on the case. As soon as this dancing thing is taken care of, I'll fix your rat problem, okay?"

But I couldn't imagine any way that Fink could fix my problem. For all we knew, somebody might have already bought my rat and taken it home and given it some awful corny name like Ratty. Just thinking about it made me feel sick.

Fink didn't sit with me at lunch that afternoon. He said he had something to take care of. I figured it had something to do with his big plan, so I didn't even ask him what he was up to. I just sat in the corner by myself, eating my sandwich and thinking about my rat.

After lunch we went to the gym for our third, and hopefully last, session with Miss Treehaven. She was waiting there for us, dressed in a purple fur cape and matching tights.

"She looks like a hairy grape," Fink snickered when we came in.

"Now that we've done a few exercises, and gotten our feet wet, so to speak," Miss Treehaven told us, "it's time to begin work on the piece you'll be doing next Friday at your performance. As you may have guessed, the theme will be emotions. Today I will be asking you to audition in pairs, one boy and one girl for each of the roles. We'll begin with *love*."

All of the girls started wildly waving their hands in the air to be picked. Miss Treehaven chose Marla.

"Just because she takes ballet, she's probably going to get the biggest part," Bethany complained.

"Well, I *am* advanced," said Marla defensively.

"Now I need a gentleman to be her partner. Any volunteers?" Miss Treehaven asked.

We all turned to Fink. He'd told us he would start the ball rolling, and it looked like the time had come to start rolling.

I saw him swallow hard, then slowly raise his hand.

"I'll do it," he said, getting up and walking over to stand next to Marla. "Ready or not, here comes love."

Our eyes were glued to him, waiting to see what he would do next.

"I'm going to play some music to put you in the mood," said Miss Treehaven, "and then I'd like for the two of you to interpret it for me."

She pushed a button on the little tape recorder she'd brought with her that day, and sappy, lovely-dovey violin music poured out into the room like syrup. Marla immediately swung into action, pointing her toes and leaping around the room, pretending to pick and gather flowers in her arms. Fink didn't waste a second. He ran over and started leaping right next to her. But instead of pointing his toes gracefully, the way Marla was, every time he leapt, Fink would stick out his back leg and trip her. Marla stumbled a few times and then stopped dancing. She was furious.

"No fair!" she shouted. "He's trying to sabotage my dancing. I can't possibly audition like this! I need another partner!"

Miss Treehaven tried to pair Danny with Marla,

but he knew what to do. He copied Fink's tripping move and added a couple of moves of his own. Marla was in a rage. Miss Treehaven stopped the music and asked them both to sit down.

"It's a conspiracy!" Marla shouted. "I demand a solo!"

"Perhaps it's the emotion that's causing the problem," said Miss Treehaven. "Let's try dancing *joy*. Any volunteers?"

This time the dancers were Bethany and David Framer. As soon as Miss Treehaven turned on the music, David started rolling around on the floor kicking his legs and barking like a dog, making it impossible for Bethany to do anything but try to protect herself from getting kicked.

Miss Treehaven seemed perplexed.

"I don't understand. You didn't dance this way yesterday," she said. "And you certainly weren't barking. Whatever has gotten into you?"

"It's not *us*," Jessie said. "It's *them*. The boys are the ones who are messing everybody up. Why do we have to be partners with them?"

"Perhaps you have a point, young lady. Let's try having just the girls dance for a moment," said Miss Treehaven as she got up and straightened her grape cape.

The boys were more than happy to move to the side and sit on the floor watching while the girls danced. Miss Treehaven had them leap and spin and skip and hop to the music, and not once did anyone run into anyone else or fall down.

"*Faboo!*" cried Miss Treehaven. "Absolutely *faboo!*"

Marla held her hands out to the sides, pointed her toes, and kept a serious look on her face the whole time she was dancing. It was sickening watching her show off, but I have to admit, she did look like she knew what she was doing.

"Brilliant!" Miss Treehaven cried as Marla skipped across the floor like a fairy. "Lovely!" she exclaimed as Jessie and Bethany floated together like butterflies. "*Faboo!*" she said as Leslie Zebak spun around hugging herself, then threw herself on the floor, looking over at Fink and sighing with her hands over her heart.

Fink looked like he was going to be sick.

After a while, Miss Treehaven clapped her hands and the girls stopped dancing. Their cheeks were all pink and they were out of breath.

"That was marvelous!" she cried. "And now that you've shown them how it's done, let's add the boys back in and give them another go at it," said Miss Treehaven. "Remember, gentlemen, light on your feet and joyous! Think of happy things — birthday parties, fireworks, splashing in the cool ocean on a hot day. Candy apples, pony rides, flying a kite in a beautiful meadow!"

"This is it," Fink whispered to us as we took the floor. "Stink like you've never stunk before."

We stunk all right. We were the opposite of graceful in every possible way. Miss Treehaven's eyes got very wide as she watched us dance, at least as wide as they could get while still holding up those eyelashes of hers. The final straw came when Mad Dog — who was stomping around to the music like an insane giant, making hideous faces and hanging his tongue out of the side of his mouth like a rabid dog — accidentally stomped on three different girls' toes at the same time and made them all cry.

Miss Treehaven turned off the music.

"That's it!" she said. "I have reached the end of my rope."

Then she threw up her hands and left the gym in a huff, her purple cape flying behind her as she went.

Fink leaned over and whispered in my ear, "I smell victory!"

Mrs. West ran after her but returned a minute later with a look on her face we'd only seen a couple of times before, when she was really, really angry about something.

"Miss Treehaven has informed me that she doesn't feel her work here is being appreciated, and so she's decided not to complete the dance workshop with our class," Mrs. West told us. "There will be no more dance classes, and since we obviously have nothing to show for all of her efforts, there will be no performance next Friday, either."

The boys all started pumping their fists in the air

and cheering. But Mrs. West glared at us so fiercely that we stopped in mid-pump.

"This is not a time to celebrate. It's disgraceful and selfish, what you've done," she said angrily. "Because of the childish behavior of you boys, our whole class has been robbed of what could have been a phenomenal experience. It's a great loss, not only for this class, but for the whole community at Jeffersonville Elementary. You ought to be ashamed of yourselves!"

Mrs. West looked at us with such disappointment that I felt really bad, even though I was relieved that I wasn't going to have to dance anymore. I like Mrs. West, and we'd let her down.

A bunch of girls were crying now — not just the ones Mad Dog had stomped on. I never take it that seriously when girls cry. I knew this girl once who lost a button off her favorite sweater, and the way she cried, you'd have thought somebody had died. They're beyond weird, I'm telling you.

"Since it's only the boys who were so *immature*," said Marla, "couldn't you ask Miss Treehaven to come back and work with just the girls? We could do the production without them, no problem. Some of us are quite advanced."

I saw Jessie roll her eyes again at Marla's bragging, but all the girls seemed to agree with her that they were better off without the boys.

"Who needs them?" asked Bethany. "Besides, I already finished making the flyer and everything."

Mrs. West shook her head.

"I'm sorry. Miss Treehaven said that unless the whole class is not only *willing* to participate but *eager* to, she can't be involved in the project any longer," said Mrs. West. "So, what about it, boys? Are you *eager* to learn how to dance?"

We all looked at Fink. Would he raise his hand? Would he tell her that the boys were *eager* to put on pink tights and skirts and dance around on a stage? I saw his arm twitch once, but in the end, he didn't raise it. How could he? I'm sure he felt bad about upsetting Mrs. West, too, but he was our leader and he knew that none of us wanted to dance.

"Can't you *make* them dance?" asked Jessie.

My mom always says, "You can lead a horse to water, but you can't make him drink." If Mrs. West had been looking for an expression to use right then, that would have been a good one, but instead she just sighed.

"It's your loss," she said. "We're going back to the classroom now. If we can't dance, we'll do fractions for the rest of the afternoon."

It looked like we had won the war. But here's something worth remembering — don't count your chickens before they're hatched.

CHAPTER EIGHT

"I feel bad about Mrs. West," I told Fink as we walked home from school that afternoon.

"Bad enough to go back and tell her you've changed your mind and you're just dying to put on a pair of pink tights and dance around in front of the whole world?" he asked.

"No, but I still feel bad," I said.

"Well, I have something that will cheer you up," said Fink. "Today at lunch I —" But we were interrupted when something sharp suddenly hit me in the back of the neck. Another of Mad Dog's spitballs.

"Hey, cut it out, Mad Dog," I said as I turned around. "It's not Tuesday anymore, you know."

But it wasn't Mad Dog, and it wasn't a spitball, either. It was Jessie and Marla and they were throwing acorns at us.

"What's the big idea?" asked Fink, ducking as an acorn whizzed past his cheek.

"It's all your fault! You two were the ringleaders, weren't you?" said Jessie. "Especially you, Fink. If you'd kept your big mouth shut, all the boys would have cooperated and Miss Treehaven wouldn't have left."

"Yeah, why did you have to be so —" But Fink interrupted Marla before she could finish her sentence.

"If you say *immature*, I swear I'm going to hire your father myself and have him sue *you* for being so annoying."

"Every girl in our class is mad at you right now," said Jessie.

"So? Why should he care what the girls think?" I asked. "All the boys think he's a hero for saving us from dancing."

"Wait a second," said Fink. "Did you say *all* the girls are mad at me?"

"Every single one," said Jessie.

"Even Leslie Zebak?" he asked.

"Especially Leslie Zebak," said Marla. "She told me she thinks you're a total jerk now. And guess what? She's right."

"And in case you're wondering," added Marla, pointing one of her stubby little fingers at me, "the same goes for you, Nat Boyd."

Marla and Jessie stormed off in their matching red Windbreakers without looking back at us.

"Well, Fink, it looks like two of your wishes came true today," I said. "No more dancing, plus I guess Leslie Zebak won't be bothering you anymore, either."

"Yeah," said Fink. But the thing is, he didn't sound nearly as happy about that as I thought he would. In fact, maybe it was my imagination, but it seemed almost as if he was worried about it.

"So, what were you saying about what you did at lunch?" I asked.

"Oh, nothing," said Fink. "I'll tell you about it later. I gotta run now."

And he took off in the opposite direction without even looking back.

Friday at school was unusually quiet. Mrs. West didn't bring up the dance thing at all, but you could tell she was still really mad. She gave us extra math homework and she didn't smile all day. The girls glared at the boys, and even though the boys were all happy not to be dancing, everybody felt a little bad about upsetting Mrs. West. Fink seemed the most upset of all. He barely said a word all day.

"You can't please everybody," I told Fink at lunch. "You made the boys happy. You should feel good about that, right?"

But he seemed preoccupied and didn't answer me.

On Saturday morning, I called Fink to see if he wanted to come over and have waffles with me and my mom, but his mom told me he'd left the house early.

"Where did he go?" I asked her.

"I'm not sure," she told me. "He was kind of mysterious about it. I thought maybe the two of you were up to something special."

"Nope," I said. "He's not with me. When he gets back, tell him to call me, okay?"

"I will, Nat," she said.

Where was Fink? And what was he up to? I waited around all morning, but he didn't call. I tried him again later in the afternoon, and this time he picked up the phone himself.

"Hey, where have you been?" I asked.

"Nowhere," he said.

"What do you mean, nowhere?" I asked. "You were *somewhere*, weren't you?"

"I meant nowhere special," he said. "What's the big deal? I'm here now, aren't I?"

This wasn't like Fink. We're best friends. We tell each other everything. Why didn't he want me to know where he'd been? The last time he'd done something without telling me about it was when he'd gone over to Miller's Swamp to try to catch me some tadpoles. Maybe he'd gone there again.

"Were you down at the swamp?" I asked.

"Nah," he said, "it's too mucky over there this time of year. You could lose your boots in that stuff. I had my clarinet lesson at one o'clock."

"Yeah, but where were you this morning? Your mom said you left the house really early," I asked.

"Yeah, so what? I left the house early. I'm allowed, aren't I?" he said.

"What's the big secret?" I asked.

"There's no secret," said Fink. "I was just hanging out this morning, that's all. Can't a guy hang out if he wants to?"

"Sure. But who were you hanging out with?" I asked.

"Me, myself, and I," he said. "Okay?"

"Okay," I said, but it felt really weird. Fink was keeping a secret from me.

"So what are you up to?" Fink asked me.

"Nothing much. You want to come over?" I asked.

"Sure," he said. "Time me."

Fink's record for the fastest time from his house to mine is fifty-seven seconds. This time it took him one minute and thirty-six seconds.

"What took you so long?" I asked when he finally got there.

"My mom starting asking me all these questions right before I left," he explained.

I had a few questions I wanted to ask him myself, but I decided to wait until it felt like the right time.

"Hey, want to go over to the school and shoot some hoops or something?" he asked me.

"Sure," I said. "I'll grab a ball. Should we bring something to eat?"

"Let's stop at the Bee Hive afterward instead," he said. "I'm in the mood for a Froozle."

On the way over to the school, Fink was quiet. I dribbled the basketball on the sidewalk as we walked. Finally I broke the silence.

"I had the weirdest dream yesterday," I told him.

"Yeah? Weirder than the one you had about Mad Dog making you bungee jump out of a tree by holding on to the back of your underwear?" Fink asked.

"Yeah, even weirder," I told him.

"Was Jessie in it this time?" Fink asked.

"Yeah, she was a big part of it," I said.

"Was she wearing the you-know-what?" Fink asked.

"Yep, she had on that dumb wedding dress. But the worst thing was, instead of a bouquet, she was walking around holding my rat," I told him.

"Your rat?" asked Fink. "Oh, you mean the one with the notched ear?"

"Yeah," I said, "and the intelligent eyes."

"You're sure that's the one you want, right?" he asked.

"I'm sure. It's the most perfect rat in the world," I said.

When we got to the school, there was nobody on the basketball court. I threw the ball to Fink and started running.

"Pass it to me and watch me dunk!" I yelled over my shoulder. "Alley-oop!"

But Fink didn't throw the ball to me. When I turned around I was surprised to see he was still standing right where I'd left him. But he wasn't alone anymore. Leslie Zebak was there with him.

I started to walk over to where they were standing

to see if Fink needed some help getting rid of her. But when he saw me coming, he held up both his hands and motioned for me to stop. When he had finished talking to her, they shook hands and she left.

"What was that all about?" I asked when Fink came over to the courts.

He tossed me the ball.

"Nothing," he said. "Let's see you dunk."

I put the ball down on the ground and sat on it.

"Okay, that's it," I said, folding my arms across my chest. "Tell me what's going on."

Fink bit his lower lip. He always does that when he's upset.

"Look," he said, "maybe there's something going on, and maybe there's not. But either way, I can't talk about it, okay?"

"What do you mean you can't talk about it?" I asked. "We tell each other everything. That's the rule."

"I know, but this is different," he said. "I promised."

"Promised who?" I asked.

"I can't tell you that, either," he said. "Come on, just drop it. Let's shoot some hoops."

"Forget it," I said. "If you're not going to tell me what's going on, I'm out of here."

I stood up and put the ball under my arm.

"Don't go," he said. "I want to tell you, I just can't."

I reached down and scratched my knee.

"Uh-oh," said Fink, pointing to my leg.

Uh-oh was right. My best friend was keeping secrets from me — did I need a better reason to be itchy?

"Look what you're doing to me," I said, scratching the back of my right knee vigorously with the toe of my left sneaker. I really was itchy, but it wasn't as bad as I was making it out to be. I was trying to make Fink feel guilty. Maybe then he'd feel he *had* to tell me the big secret, whatever it was.

"I'm sorry," he said. "I don't mean to be making you itch. I can't help it. I promised not to tell. And if I tell, well — it's complicated, okay?"

"No, it's not okay. Who did you promise?" I asked. "Leslie Zebak? Is that what you guys were talking about before over there? Was she telling you to keep secrets from me?"

Fink just stood there hanging his head.

"I'm sorry," he said softly. "I can't tell you."

Now I was mad.

"Okay, fine," I said, "don't tell me. But don't expect me to tell you any of my secrets anymore. And don't expect me to stay best friends with you, either. Best friends don't keep secrets from each other, in case you forgot."

I walked away then. I half expected him to chase after me, but he didn't. I left him standing on the basketball court watching me go. No trip to Washington, no rat, and now, no best friend, either. Like I said earlier, sometimes life really stinks.

CHAPTER NINE

I didn't see Fink at all on Sunday, and I didn't call him, either. I was still mad at him, and if anybody was going to call or make the effort to make up, it was going to have to be him.

Monday morning he wasn't waiting on the corner to walk to school with me the way he usually did, so I walked by myself. When I got to class, I was surprised to see Fink already there, standing next to Mrs. West's desk. And who was standing right beside him? None other than Leslie Zebak. Fink looked over and when he saw me, he started to raise his hand like he was going to wave to me, but then Leslie gave him this look, and he put his hand down and turned away.

I felt mad all over again. My best friend was taking orders from a girl all of a sudden. That is, my *former* best friend.

When Fink and Leslie finished talking to Mrs. West, she nodded and smiled and patted Fink on the shoulder. Whatever it was he had just told her had obviously made her happy. Fink and Leslie went and sat down at their desks.

"Class, I have something important to discuss with you this morning," Mrs. West said right after she took attendance. "Apparently a bit of soul-searching went on over the weekend and it's been suggested to me that in light of this, it might be worthwhile for us to revote on the issue of whether the boys would like to participate in Miss Treehaven's dance project, after all."

What was she talking about? Which of us did she think had changed our minds over the weekend about dancing? Certainly not me! Things were bad enough without adding *that* back into the mix.

"Now, can we please have a show of hands for

those of you who would like to have Miss Treehaven return to finish the dance project?" Mrs. West asked.

All the girls put their hands up immediately. The boys all turned to Fink, including me, even though I was mad at him. He was still our leader in this department, after all. He sat there for a second and then, to my utter amazement, he wiped his palm on his pants and put his hand up. I couldn't believe my eyes! Our leader, the one who only a few days ago had told us we had to stand up for ourselves and refuse to be humiliated in public, was raising his hand! Fink was voting to dance!

"What are you doing?" Jeremy whispered to Fink. "Have you lost your mind?"

"Yeah, Fink," added Danny, "we don't want to dance. Put your hand down before somebody takes you seriously."

Everybody was grumbling and whispering to Fink, but he either didn't hear them or he didn't care, because he didn't lower his hand. He just looked straight ahead and stuck it even higher in the air. What was going on? Had Leslie Zebak brainwashed Fink into wanting to dance? *Was that possible?*

People always say that Fink is one of those people who has what they call leadership qualities. I guess it's really true, because I'm positive there wasn't one boy in there who had any desire to lay eyes on Miss Treehaven again, let alone dance with her. But because Fink had his hand up, one by one, all the other boys began to raise their hands, too. All except Mad Dog and me, that is. We seemed to be the only ones who hadn't gone completely insane.

"Majority rules!" shouted Jessie with glee, looking at all the hands in the air.

"I'm afraid not in this case, Miss Kornblume," said Mrs. West. "Miss Treehaven made it very clear that one hundred percent of the class had to be wholeheartedly in favor of the dance project or she would not return. As you can see, we are two votes short of unanimous."

"Come on, you guys," said Jessie. "Raise your hands. Pretty please with sugar on top."

All the girls started pleading with us like that. I

had to cover my ears to block out the sound of their begging.

"Come on," Marla whined. "Put your hands up."

"No way. No how. I am *not* going to vote yes to wearing a tutu, no matter what anybody says!" Mad Dog shouted above the noise.

"Quiet!" Mrs. West shouted. "Did I hear that right, Mr. Ditmeyer? Did you just say that the reason you won't vote yes is that you don't want to wear a tutu?"

"That's right," said Mad Dog. "I refuse to wear a skirt. And there isn't anybody in this room who's gonna make me, either."

He slowly looked around the room, glaring at us, daring us to try.

"What on earth gave you the idea you would have to wear a tutu, Mr. Ditmeyer?" Mrs. West asked.

Mad Dog pointed at Fink.

"He told us so," he said.

"Hey, don't blame me, Mad Dog. Marla and Jessie are the ones who told me," said Fink. "I was only passing along the facts. They said we had to wear pink tights and naked leotards and if we were *lucky*, tutus."

Mrs. West's mouth turned into a thin straight line and she put her hands on her hips. We'd all seen the look before.

"Girls, is this true? Did you tell the boys they would have to wear tights and tutus when they danced?" she asked.

One good thing about Marla and Jessie both being redheads is that their skin is really pale, and when they blush, there's no missing it. They were both turning beet red. It was obvious they were guilty.

"Well?" said Mrs. West, looking from one of the girls to the other.

"We might have," said Jessie softly.

"Yeah, we might have," echoed Marla. "By accident."

"I don't believe there was anything accidental about it," said Mrs. West. "And it certainly explains a lot."

"We're sorry," Jessie said. "We were only kidding." Marla nodded.

"We didn't think they'd believe us," she said. "Everybody knows boys don't ever wear tutus."

"What about the pink tights?" asked Danny warily.

"Although men do wear tights for some types of dancing, in my experience they are rarely pink," explained Mrs. West. "And in the type of modern dancing that we would be doing with Miss Treehaven, everyone, boys and girls alike, would be wearing regular clothes. Her dancers are always dressed that way."

Okay, so that was good. At least we wouldn't have to wear tights and tutus. But wait a second! Tutus or not, the whole idea was that we weren't supposed to have to dance at all. That's what we'd decided, wasn't it? And that's what we'd achieved already. So why was Fink trying to make us change our minds all of a sudden?

"Now that we've cleared up that misunderstanding, let's vote once more. How many of you would like to have Miss Treehaven return?" Mrs. West asked.

The same thing happened again. The girls' hands all shot up, then Fink voted yes and the rest of the boys reluctantly followed his lead. This time, unbelievable as it was, Mad Dog voted yes, too.

"You'd better know what you're doing, Finky boy," I heard him grumble under his breath. "Or you're toast."

"Well, Mr. Boyd," said Mrs. West, "looks like it's up to you. Your vote is going to swing this thing one way or the other."

I reached down and scratched my knee, which had been growing itchier and itchier over the past few minutes. Then I looked around. Everyone was staring at me. I felt like the whole world had gone crazy and left me behind. This was one of those moments when you turn to your best friend for help. Only I couldn't. I didn't have one anymore.

Mrs. West said she would give me a little more time to think about my decision and that she'd take the final vote at the end of the day. Then she started writing math problems on the board. I was relieved not to be on the spot for the moment, but I couldn't concentrate at all. Nothing made sense anymore. Why was Fink acting so weird? I looked over in his direction, and things suddenly got even weirder.

He was passing a note to Leslie Zebak! At first I

thought it was my imagination. But then, as I watched, she wrote something on his note and passed it back. Then he wrote something and passed it back to her. I never would have believed it if I hadn't seen it with my own eyes.

Then something really disturbing dawned on me. The only kind of notes Fink had ever gotten from Leslie Zebak were love notes. Was Fink writing love notes to her now, too? The idea was mind-boggling. Now I really couldn't concentrate on my math. Was it possible? Had I really lost my best friend *to a girl?*

When the lunch bell rang, everybody got up and left the room in a hurry. It was Monday — pizza day in the cafeteria — and if you got there early, you might stand a chance of getting seconds. I didn't care about pizza, though. I wasn't hungry. Nothing kills your appetite quicker than seeing your best friend writing love notes to a girl, right in front of your face.

"Is there something troubling you, Mr. Boyd?" Mrs. West asked.

I'd been so wrapped up in my thoughts that I hadn't noticed her standing beside my desk.

"Oh, no. I'm fine," I said. "Just a little tired, I guess."
I tried to fake a yawn to make it seem believable.

"Do you mind if I ask you something?" she asked. "I was wondering why you didn't follow Mr. Fink's lead this morning. You two are usually thick as thieves. I've never known you not to go along with each other's plans in the past."

I didn't know what to say. Of course she was right. Fink and I had always voted the same way on everything. But I didn't feel like telling Mrs. West that Fink was keeping secrets, or about the note passing with Leslie Zebak. She doesn't allow note passing in class, and even though I was mad at Fink, I didn't see any point in trying to get him in trouble.

"I guess maybe Fink just likes dancing better than I do," I said.

Mrs. West looked like she was going to say something else, but then she didn't. Maybe she could tell I really didn't want to talk about it.

"Are you going to get some pizza, Mr. Boyd?" she asked.

"I'm not really hungry today," I told her. "Is it okay if I stay in here and work on those math problems? I didn't quite finish."

"Suit yourself," she said. "Personally, I'm in a pizza kind of mood."

Mrs. West left me alone in the classroom. I was about to copy down one of the problems off the board when out of the corner of my eye I noticed something white on the floor near Fink's desk. It was the note from Leslie! He must have dropped it.

I know you're not supposed to read other people's mail, but I didn't care. I pounced on the paper, quickly unfolding the tiny square and revealing the messages they'd sent to each other. I recognized Fink's handwriting easily. He'd written:

Can I please tell Nat what's going on?

And in her girly cursive she'd written back:

No! You promised.

Then he'd written:

Okay. Whatever you say. This is really important to me.

Then she'd written:

Has anybody ever told you that you have a really cute nose?

I felt sick. My worst fears had been confirmed. The secret Fink was keeping from me was that he was in love with Leslie. I read the note again. *This is really important to me,* he had written. I had the proof right there in my hand. Fink had deserted me for Leslie Zebak. She was more important to him now than I was. Boy, did that hurt.

When everyone came back in from lunch, I could smell the pizza on their breath. My stomach grumbled and I realized I was hungry, even though I was upset. As Fink passed my desk, he tripped over his own feet and stopped himself from falling by grabbing onto my sleeve.

"Hey, watch it!" I said, pushing him off of me. I didn't want him anywhere near me. The traitor.

"Sorry," he said, and kept walking toward his desk.

I noticed Leslie watching him very carefully. Then I noticed something else. A folded square of white paper in my lap. It wasn't the note I'd found on the floor. I'd put that in my desk. This was a new note from Fink.

I was dying to open it and read it, but I was afraid Mrs. West might see, so I stuck it between the pages of my math book and waited for the right moment. Finally I got my chance when the principal came in to talk to Mrs. West about something for a minute.

While she was distracted, I quickly opened the note and read it. It was very short. He'd written:

Trust me. Vote yes.

That was it, no explanation for why he was writing love notes to Leslie Zebak or keeping secrets from me or signing us all up for dance lessons with a crazy woman. Just: *Trust me. Vote yes.*

I put the note away and watched the second hand go slowly around the clock, minute by minute, for the rest of the afternoon. Finally, at five minutes to three, Mrs. West stood up and said it was time for the final vote.

"All in favor of inviting Tallulah Treehaven to return, please raise your hands," she told us.

I looked over at Fink. Boyd Fink, who'd known me, Nat Boyd, since kindergarten. We'd made friends the first day of school on account of us sharing the same name, and we'd pretty much been best friends ever since. He knew about my secret dreams of Jessie in the wedding dress, and I knew he still slept with a teddy bear he'd had since he was a baby. We'd had millions of sleepovers together, eaten hundreds of pickles sitting in the tree in my backyard, played countless games of A or B? and Jinx on Froozles.

Trust me. Vote yes.

I wasn't sure I was doing the right thing, but I closed my eyes and raised my hand anyway.

CHAPTER TEN

The dismissal bell rang and everybody packed up their backpacks and grabbed their jackets off the hooks in the closets before rushing out into the crowded hall. Somehow my jacket had gotten pulled off the hook by accident and kicked across the floor in the jumble of feet. By the time I got it and brushed all the shoeprints off it, everybody else had left. Just as I was finally about to go, Mrs. West stopped me at the door.

"I'm glad you decided to change your vote," she said.

"Thanks," I said, which I know sounds kind of lame, but I couldn't think of anything else to say right then. All I wanted was to get out of there and find

Fink so he could explain what was going on. I figured he would wait around for me outside, and we'd talk and walk home together. I'd trusted him and voted yes because of his note, now he owed me an explanation.

Mrs. West let me go, but when I got outside, Fink was nowhere in sight. Marla and Jessie were, though.

"It's a good thing you voted yes," said Jessie.

"Yeah," said Marla. "Otherwise . . ."

"Otherwise what?" I said. "Go ahead, finish your sentence. I'd just love to know what you think you could do to me that would be any worse than what's already happened."

Jessie grabbed Marla by the hand and yanked on her arm.

"Come on," she said. "Let's get away from this loser before it rubs off on us."

"Loser?" I said. "*Me?* I think maybe you'd better take a look in the mirror, Corn Bloomers. I'm not the one being twinsy-pinsy with my best friend all the time."

"Maybe that's because you don't have a best friend anymore," said Jessie.

Where was Fink now, when I needed him most? I looked around. Maybe I'd missed him; maybe he was over on the basketball court or something. No such luck. Fink was nowhere in sight.

"Whatcha looking for, Nat? Lose something?" said Marla. "Like maybe your *best friend*?"

"What do you know about it?" I said angrily.

"I know more than you do," said Marla. "I know where my best friend is — do you?"

I couldn't argue with that. I didn't know where Fink was. I didn't know why he'd voted to dance or why he was writing notes to Leslie Zebak. I didn't know anything — including what to say to Jessie and Marla. So I just left without saying anything.

I stopped at the Bee Hive on the way home hoping maybe I'd find Fink, but the only one I recognized there was Mad Dog.

"Hey, worm," he called out to me.

Nice. Nothing like being insulted when you're down.

"What do you want, Mad Dog? 'Cause if you plan on creaming me, do me a favor and just get it over with, will you?" I said. "I can't take any more suspense at the moment."

"What's with you?" he asked. "I just wanted to ask you what your little friend was up to today making us vote for bringing back the bird lady."

"How should I know what he was up to?" I said. "I'm not the boss of him. If you want to know, why don't you ask him yourself?"

"Maybe I'll do that," he said. "I know where to find him."

"You do?" I asked. "You know where Fink is right now?"

"Yep," he said.

"Where is he, then?" I asked.

"You mean you don't know?" he asked.

"I'm sure he told me. I just forgot," I said, trying to cover. "So why don't you remind me where he is, okay?"

"How much is it worth to you to be *reminded*?" asked Mad Dog. "I don't just give out information for free, you know."

"What do you want?" I asked.

"How about a vanilla Froozle," he said.

"Forget it," I told him. "I'm not wasting my money on Froozles for you. I can find Fink for myself; he probably just went home."

"No, he didn't," said Mad Dog.

I really did want to know where Fink was, but if I bought a Froozle for Mad Dog, I'd have to cut into my rat money. I knew it was unrealistic to think I could ever raise enough money to buy the cage and all the other stuff I needed for it, but I still wasn't ready to give up the money I'd actually managed to save.

"Okay, fine," I said. "Don't tell me if you don't want to. See if I care."

I turned and started to walk away.

"Wait," said Mad Dog. "Got any gum?"

I happened to have a pack of sugarless gum in my backpack. My mom finally gave up on trying to make me brush my teeth after lunch at school and told me to chew a piece of sugarless gum after I ate instead. I unzipped the front pouch and showed him the pack.

"This is all I've got. Take it or leave it," I told him.

He reached for the gum.

"Follow me," he told me.

Mad Dog is taller than me and his legs are about twice as long as mine. As he walked, I trotted along behind him like a puppy, doing my best to keep up with him.

"Where are we going?" I asked.

"You'll see," he told me.

"Look, I gave you the gum. Tell me where he is," I said.

Mad Dog stopped walking and turned and glared down at me.

"You gave me *sugarless* gum," he sneered. "For sugarless gum, you don't get to ask questions. You just get to zip your lip and follow me there. Understand?"

I nodded. What else could I do? I was out of gum and Mad Dog was my only hope of finding Fink at the moment. I couldn't afford to make him mad and I was determined to find out why Fink had written me that note.

When we turned down a street called Mulberry, Mad Dog slowed down.

"It's one of these houses," he said.

"Whose house is it?" I asked. "I don't know anybody who lives here."

"Yes, you do," he said.

"Who?" I asked.

He didn't answer; he just kept walking. Finally he stopped in front of a red house with white shutters and a black mailbox on a post at the end of the driveway. My heart sank when I saw the name written in white block print across the side. ZEBAK.

"This is it," he said, pointing up at the house. "He's in there. You going in?"

I shook my head. I didn't want to see Fink in there making goo-goo eyes at Leslie. Just the thought of it made me feel sad and really, really lonely.

Trust me.

Yeah, right. Suddenly, I understood. He'd made me vote for the dancing because he'd wanted to make Leslie happy. She'd asked him to make us vote for the dancing because *she* wanted to dance. That's what this was all about. Fink had sacrificed all the boys — even me — so he wouldn't have to disappoint Leslie Zebak.

"Hey, where are you going?" asked Mad Dog as I turned and headed back the way we'd come from.

I shrugged. I didn't know where I was going. All I knew was I had to get away from there fast — before Mad Dog saw the tears in my eyes.

CHAPTER ELEVEN

The next day at school, Tallulah Treehaven was waiting for us after lunch. She told us that she was very excited to be back, and happy that we'd decided we wanted to dance. She said that we would be working on our dance very hard for the next three afternoons and then putting on the performance on Friday at an assembly in the auditorium.

"There won't be time to send out the flyers now, so everybody will have to take them home in their backpacks this afternoon, okay?" Bethany told us.

"We don't have much time to prepare, but I'm sure if you put your minds, and especially your bodies to it, you'll all be absolutely *faboo!*" Miss Treehaven said.

Then she told us that she'd been giving quite a lot of thought to the theme of the dance we would be doing.

"Will *love* still be in it?" asked Marla. "I think I deserve another audition for that."

"No," explained Miss Treehaven. "It didn't seem that love or any of the other emotions really resonated with the gentlemen, so instead I've decided on a totally new concept — one that I hope will please everyone, particularly the boys. The new theme is *sports*."

"For real?" asked David Framer, the fastest runner in the whole sixth grade. "Sports? You mean, like track?"

"Track, football, hockey, baseball, wherever your passion lies," said Miss Treehaven happily.

All the boys started buzzing. That Miss Treehaven was smarter than we'd given her credit for. I'm sure she knew that *sports* is kind of a magic word when it comes to boys. Obviously it was a good theme if she wanted to get the boys excited about the project. The girls, however, were a lot less enthusiastic. Marla was the first to raise her hand.

"I thought you said modern dance was about interpreting emotions," she said with a pout. "Football isn't emotional. It's boring and violent."

"What about ice-skating and swimming and diving and soccer? Are those boring, too?" asked Miss Treehaven.

"How are we supposed to dance swimming?" somebody asked. "There's no pool in the auditorium."

"Maybe not, but there's an ocean in motion in your soul," said Miss Treehaven and she began to "swim" around the room, moving her arms and legs in a way that made her look like she was underwater.

"Can we wear team uniforms when we dance?" asked Mad Dog.

"Absolutely," said Miss Treehaven. "I think that would be absolutely *faboo*!"

"My football jersey's got mad cool blood on it from one of my awesome tackles," said Mad Dog.

Several of the girls made squeamish sounds, but

Jeremy, who happens to play on Mad Dog's football team, snorted.

"That's ketchup on your jersey, Mad Dog," he said. "I saw you smear it on there at the Bee Hive after practice last week."

"If we're dancing ice-skating, but we don't happen to have ice-skating skirts, would it be okay if Jessie and I wore tutus?" asked Marla.

"Let's not worry about the outside anymore right now," said Miss Treehaven. "We need to turn our focus to what's on the inside."

The problem was, I didn't want to focus on what was going on inside me right then. I was in pain. All I could think about was Fink. For the second day in a row, we hadn't walked to school together. In the yard before the first bell, he'd made a point of keeping as far away from me as possible. And at lunch, I'd seen him sitting at a table in the corner with Leslie Zebak. This was worse than any nightmare I'd ever had. This was real. How was I going to survive being in this pain and having to dance at the same time?

The funny thing is, over the next three days, something unexpected happened. All morning long, I'd sit in class moping and seething and feeling bummed out about Fink, but (here's the unexpected part) when Tallulah Treehaven showed up in the afternoon, I actually began looking forward to the dancing. It was a lot better without the mushy love music. Instead of making me crazy, dancing was about the only thing that helped me feel better.

I had chosen soccer as my sport since I love soccer and I'm pretty good at it, too. My dance consisted of kicking an imaginary ball around the room. It doesn't sound like much of a dance, but what made it especially satisfying was that every time I kicked the ball, I thought about Fink and our friendship and about how he'd taken advantage of my trust.

Miss Treehaven would play tapes of music with plenty of drums and trumpets and crashing cymbals, and I would close my eyes and kick harder and harder, until I was sweating and the angry feelings felt like they were shooting out of my feet.

"*Faboo*, Nathaniel! Such passion!" Miss Treehaven would cry. "Such feeling! Such emotion!"

I wasn't the only one who seemed to be enjoying the dancing. Of course, the girls were all loving it. They were swimming and skating and doing all kinds of graceful junk with their hands and feet. But the boys were into it, too. David Framer came up with this way of running in slow motion that was very cool, and even Mad Dog looked pretty good tackling invisible opponents and doing touchdown dances with his arms over his head and his knees pumping high. I made a point of not watching what Fink was doing. I didn't even want to know.

Mrs. West was thrilled with us.

"I knew you wouldn't let me down, and some of you," she was looking at me when she said this part, "have even surpassed my wildest expectations. I'm so glad you changed your minds."

I would have felt good about that if I hadn't been feeling so bad about Fink. I was okay when I was dancing, but the rest of the time I was still bummed out. I hated walking to school alone. I missed talking to Fink on the phone and just being around him in general. I'd started eating lunch with Jeremy and Danny, but all they were interested in talking about was chess club and some TV show Fink and I always used to make fun of for being babyish.

I wished more than ever that I had a rat to go home to after school. Someone to talk to and hang out with, even if it was only a rodent. Instead, I'd go home and stare at Hercules swimming in his bowl, or sit up in my tree alone, or surf the Web for hairless rat sites where I could at least read about what great pets they made.

When Friday rolled around, Miss Treehaven insisted we were ready for the dance performance. She said we were all dancing beautifully, and that our inner selves were shining through. I was pretty sure that an audience would think we looked more like a bunch of kids running around on a playground, but it didn't really matter. The dance was only going to last about five minutes.

Everyone came to school wearing some sort of sports outfit. I wore my soccer uniform, and Mad Dog had on his football gear, including the ketchupy jersey and a helmet with a disgusting, spitty mouthguard hanging off the front of it. Jessie and Marla, of course, had on matching tutus, and they'd taped strips of aluminum foil to the sides of their shoes to look like skate blades.

The auditorium was packed. My mom was there, sitting way in the back in case her cell phone rang and she had to leave for an orthodontic emergency. I had given her the flyer and told her that she could come, but only after she promised not to bring the video camera with her to the performance.

Before we danced, Miss Treehaven made a little speech about how much she'd enjoyed working with us and what good sports we all were (ha-ha), and then Mrs. West gave her a bouquet of roses from the class.

When the applause died down, Miss Treehaven pressed the button on her tape recorder and the performance began.

Everything was going fine, I was kicking away at my imaginary ball as usual, until I happened to look over and see Fink. Like I said, I had made a point of not paying any attention to him during the rehearsals, so I had no idea what sport he had chosen. Fink doesn't even play sports. His mom and dad won't let him because they're afraid he might hurt himself. He wasn't wearing a uniform like everybody else; instead he was dressed all in brown and hanging out of the back of his pants was what looked like a bunch of black hair. Leslie Zebak was right behind him wearing a red jacket, white pants, and black rubber rain boots. It was clear from the way they were dancing close to each other that they were partners, but I wasn't sure what they were doing.

At first I thought that Fink was running, and Leslie was chasing him, like they were having a race or playing tag or something. Suddenly I realized that Leslie was supposed to be a jockey and Fink was her horse. *Her horse.* That just made me furious! Fink and I have made fun of the girls for playing horse on the playground for years. And now there he was, bobbing his horse head just the way they did. What a traitor!

Now, you may not believe this, but what happened next was an accident. I'm not a bad person; I'm not mean. It's just that seeing Fink playing horsie with Leslie made my knee itch. I didn't want to start scratching myself onstage right there in front of everybody, so instead I closed my eyes and kicked my imaginary ball as hard as I could. At least, I meant to kick my ball. But when I kicked, instead of air, my foot kicked something hard, and when I opened my eyes Fink was lying on the floor in front of me, holding his side and writhing in horrible pain.

What had I done?

CHAPTER TWELVE

I don't even remember how the dance ended. I think Miss Treehaven just turned off the tape recorder and we all stood there watching, while two fathers from the audience came and carried Fink off the stage and down to the nurse's office. My mom came over to me and put her arm around my shoulder.

"Don't feel bad, honey. I'm sure Boyd knows it was an accident," she said.

I wasn't so sure he knew that.

"Why did you do that, you big creep?" Leslie Zebak asked me, looking as though she was about to cry. "Don't you know he was only doing all this because of you?"

"What do you mean, because of me? What are you talking about?" I asked, and my voice shook I was so upset.

But before she could answer, Miss Treehaven came over, bent down in front of me, and put her face really close to mine. The heat of the spotlights on the stage, plus all the nervous energy flying around, must have done something to the glue holding her tarantula eyelashes on, because one of them suddenly curled up like a spring and fell off. I reached out and caught it.

"Here you go," I said as I handed it back to her.

"You mustn't feel badly about your friend, Nathaniel," she said softly. "You were lost in the moment, that's all." Then she looked up at my mother. "Your son is a very passionate dancer, you know."

"Apparently so," said my mother.

I was still trying to figure out what Leslie Zebak had meant about Fink doing all this stuff because of me. What stuff was she talking about? Writing love notes? Playing horsie? I didn't know why he was doing it, but it certainly wasn't because of me.

Tallulah Treehaven started talking to my mother

about some summer dance program she thought I might enjoy, so I slipped away while I had the chance. I had to find Fink and make sure he was okay.

I found him lying on a cot in the nurse's office with an ice pack on his side, looking at his watch.

"What took you so long?" he said when I walked in.

"What do you mean?" I asked.

"I timed you. It took you five minutes and thirty-two seconds to get here," he said.

"What are you talking about? Why did you time me?" I said. "Wait, don't answer that. I've got more important questions to ask you. First of all, are you okay?"

"Yeah," he said. "The nurse says nothing's broken, but I'll probably be sore for a while. That was some kick."

"I'm really sorry," I said.

"Me too," he said. "I wanted to tell you so bad, but the deal was if I told you before the dance, then I couldn't have the stuff."

"What stuff? What are you talking about?" I said.

"Rat stuff," he said.

"Rat stuff?" I asked.

"Yeah, Leslie Zebak's got rat stuff, and she told me if I danced with her at the performance, she'd give it to you for your rat," Fink explained.

My head was spinning.

"You mean this whole thing really was because of me?" I said.

"Yep," said Fink. "I would have told you if I could, but part of the deal was it had to be a secret, 'cause Leslie was afraid if the guys found out, they wouldn't be willing to dance just so you could get rat stuff. That's why I wrote you the note, so you wouldn't mess up the deal by refusing to let Tallulah Treehaven come back."

"Hey, you finally learned her name," I said.

"Yeah, I guess I did," said Fink.

"So, can I ask you something?" I asked. "Is Leslie Zebak your girlfriend now?"

"Are you nuts?" asked Fink, pushing himself up on one elbow and then grimacing with pain. "How could you even think something like that?"

"What was I supposed to think? You were writing

her notes and eating lunch with her, and Mad Dog told me you even went over to her house," I said.

"Yeah, to check out the rat stuff. I wanted to make sure it was for real, Nat-o," said Fink.

It's amazing how one little word can make a person feel so good. Fink calling me "Nat-o" again made everything right.

"What are you smiling about?" asked Fink.

I didn't want to embarrass him by getting all emotional about how worried I'd been about losing my friend, not to mention thinking maybe I'd broken his ribs. So I just said, "I'm smiling because for the first time in a long time, my knee isn't itching."

The nurse came in and told Fink it was okay for him to go home.

"My mom went out to the parking lot to get the car," he told me. "She's probably waiting out front now. Do you want a ride?"

"Sure," I said. "Let me just go tell my mom."

On the way home, Fink asked his mom if she'd be willing to drop us off at Leslie Zebak's house to pick something up.

"Oh, Leslie was the cute little jockey in the show today, right?" asked Mrs. Fink.

"Right, except for the part about her being cute," said Fink.

As we pulled into the Zebak driveway on Mulberry Street, it seemed like a million years ago that I had stood there with Mad Dog, feeling like I'd lost my best friend in the world. The garage door was open and Leslie was in there, still in her jockey costume, putting stuff into a big cardboard box. Mrs. Fink let us out and drove away.

"You know," Leslie said as soon as we walked into the garage, "technically, I shouldn't have to give you this stuff since you didn't do the whole dance with me."

"Come on, Leslie," said Fink. "That wasn't the deal, and you know it. It's not my fault Nat-o kicked your horse in the ribs and stopped the show. Fork over the rat stuff."

"Okay, fine," said Leslie. "But you don't have to be mean about it. I'm giving you all this great stuff; the least you could do is be nice to me about it."

"I guess you're right," said Fink. "I'll try. But if

136

you want me to be nice to you, you've got to stop writing me those love notes, okay?"

"No problem," said Leslie. "Besides, I don't really like you that much anymore. I've got a crush on someone else now. Someone more sensitive and emotional."

"Great!" said Fink. "Whoever he is, tell him I say thanks!"

We helped Leslie finish loading the rat stuff into the box. There was a large glass aquarium, a water bottle, a food dish, an exercise wheel, and a package of rat food.

"There's a big bag of cedar chips around here someplace, too," she said, digging around in the corner of the garage behind the garden tools. "Here it is."

"Are you sure you don't need any of this stuff anymore?" I asked her, taking the bag of wood chips from her.

"I'm sure," she said. "Mr. Nibbles lives in a hutch my dad built for him out in the backyard, and he's too big to use a wheel. Do you want to see him? He's really cute."

"No. We gotta go," said Fink.

"Maybe some other time, Leslie," I said. "And thanks a lot for all the stuff."

"Sure," she said. "Anytime, Nat."

We carried all the rat stuff back to my house and took it up to my room. I washed out the tank and put cedar chips in it. Then I filled the water bottle and the food dish and set the wheel in the cage.

"All you need now is the rat," said Fink.

"I've still got the money. Mad Dog tried to con me into buying him a Froozle, but I gave him gum instead," I said. "But, do you think that really good rat is still going to be there?"

"It was yesterday," said Fink.

"How do you know?" I asked.

"I've been calling the guy to check on it every day," Fink told me.

"You have? You're the best, Fink," I said.

"It's about time you noticed," said Fink.

"Don't be dumb," I said.

"Pick a plum," said Fink.

"Pick your nose," I said.

"Eat a hose," he said.

"Eat my socks," I said.

"You know what?" said Fink. "I think maybe you were right; we have outgrown this game."

"I don't care. If you want to play it, I'll do it for as long as you want," I told him. And I would have, too.

CHAPTER THIRTEEN

We went to Purr-fect Pets on Saturday morning and got there right as it was opening.

"You're the one who's been calling every day about the rat, right?" said the manager as he unlocked the door and let us in.

"Yeah, we want the notch-eared, bald one with the intelligent eyes," said Fink.

"Yes, I remember. Did you find a way to raise the extra money for the equipment?" asked the manager.

"You know what they say," I told him. "Where there's a will, there's a way."

"Which one is it, now?" asked the manager. "That little one by the food dish?"

I peered into the cage. That was my rat all right.

"It's a female," he said. "You okay with that?"

"What do you think, Fink?" I asked.

"Real girls are disgusting, but I guess bald rat girls are okay," he said. "They don't write love notes or make you play horsie, do they?"

The manager tilted his head at that, like he wasn't quite sure if Fink was joking or not.

"I've never heard of a rat learning to write, but they are pretty doggone smart. I wouldn't put anything past them," he said.

I paid for the rat, and Fink and I carefully carried her home in a cardboard box. When we put her in the glass tank, at first she seemed a little nervous, but pretty soon she took a sip of water, and then a nibble of food, and before long she was running happily in her wheel with her long pink tail curling up over her back so it wouldn't get caught.

"You want to hold her?" I asked Fink.

"Not yet," he said. "Don't laugh, but she kind of creeps me out. She's just so, so *bald*."

"You like your Uncle Barry and he's bald," I said.

"Oh, please don't mention Uncle Barry. He's mad at me at the moment," Fink said.

"Why?" I asked.

"Remember the tail on my horse costume?" asked Fink.

"Yeah, it was black and hairy-looking," I said.

"That's because it was hair. Uncle Barry's hair, to be exact," Fink said. "He and my Aunt Jane have been staying at our house this week, and I borrowed his rug to use as my tail. He was pretty upset when he found out."

I laughed and carefully reached in and took out my rat so that I could hold her in my lap. She put her head up and sniffed at me.

"Look at her. She's so cute," I said. "Look at her beautiful pink eyes."

"I guess she is kind of cute," said Fink, reaching over and gently stroking her back with one finger. "What are you going to name her, anyway?"

"I'm not sure. Got any suggestions?" I asked.

"How about Cue Ball?" said Fink.

"Why Cue Ball?" I asked.

"Hey, I thought you were the big expression expert. Haven't you ever heard someone say 'He's bald as a cue ball'?" Fink asked.

"Oh, I get it. But Cue Ball's not a good enough name for her," I said. "She needs a better name. Something really, you know, *faboo!*"

Fink and I looked at each other and smiled.

"Tallulah!" we both shouted at the same time.

"Jinx on Froozles!" I yelled, punching Fink in the arm.

"Hey, you finally won!" said Fink.

And he was right. I was a winner. I had my best friend back, and the most perfect pet in the world. Everything was perfect.

Well — almost.

Monday morning when Fink and I got to school, there was a little surprise waiting for me in my mailbox.

"I'd know that smell anywhere," said Fink, wrinkling up his nose and sniffing the air. "That's pure Zebak."

Sure enough, there was a note from Leslie in my box and here's what it said:

Roses are red

Violets are blue

And I have a crush on

Y – O – U.

P.S. Has anybody ever told you that your dancing is very emotional?

"What am I going to do?" I asked. "Leslie's after *me* now."

"Don't worry," said Fink. "I know how to handle this."

"Are you sure?" I asked.

"Don't you trust me, Nat-o?" he asked me.

I looked at my friend. My best friend in the whole world.

"Do I trust you, Fink?" I asked. "Absolutely!"

NAT'S MOM'S CORNY EXPRESSIONS

Do you remember reading these expressions?
Can you finish them? Look back through the book.
When you find the saying, fill in the blank lines.
Jot down the page number, too!

You _____ what you _____.   _____

A _____ cannot change his _____.   _____

If you can't stand the _____, get out
of the _____.   _____

There's _____ in _____.   _____

Don't count your _____ before
they're _____.   _____

You can lead a horse to _____, but you can't make him _____. _____

Where there's a _____, there's a _____. _____

ABOUT THE AUTHOR

Sarah Weeks has written numerous picture books and novels, including *Mrs. McNosh Hangs up Her Wash; Two Eggs, Please; Follow the Moon;* and the popular *Regular Guy* series for middle-grade readers. *My Guy*, the third in that series, is currently in production at Disney for a feature-length, live-action film.

Ms. Weeks is a singer/songwriter as well as an author. Many of her books, such as *Angel Face, Crocodile Smile,* and *Without You,* include CDs of her original songs. She visits many schools and libraries throughout the country every year, speaking at assemblies and serving as author-in-residence. She lives in New York City with her two teenage sons.

Other books in this series: